MOLLS LIKE IT HOT

ALSO BY DARREN DASH

MIDSUMMER'S BOTTOM

"A clever and kinky theatrical romp with a big heart." **Kirkus — a Recommended Read.**

"rude, naughty, outrageous, and very funny... a delight for the devotee of Shakespearean comedy." **Indie Reader .**

"I think I've found my favorite book of 2018. *Midsummer's Bottom* is Darren Dash at his best and most inventive form." **Scare Tissue.**

"*Midsummer's Bottom* is one of the most entertaining novels of the year. Light-hearted and humorous escapism doesn't get any better than this." **Rising Shadow.**

"Shakespeare fans in particular will find the atmosphere and humor exquisite. While they stay true to some of the Bard's ironic contentions and satirical approaches, they also add embellishments unique to Darren Dash's style and contemporary approach to Midsummer's spectacles." **Midwest Book Review.**

AN OTHER PLACE

"*An Other Place* sees an imaginative writer at the top of his craft. 9/10 stars." **Starburst.**

"This is, by far, the best book of 2016. Possibly the best book of this decade. The bastard love child of Kafka and Rod Serling." **Kelly Smith Reviews.**

"Darren Dash has opened a new artery of terror… hints of *The Twilight Zone*, *Pines*, and *Station Eleven*." **The Literary Connoisseur.**

"Lewis Carroll, L. Frank Baum, and Brett Easton Ellis may have written some weird stuff, but *An Other Place* tops all of it in terms of re-readability and overall scope." **Dread Central.**

4/5 stars — **SFX.**

A Recommended Read – **Kirkus.**

THE EVIL AND THE PURE

"The book flaunts the grim panache of a London crime saga, and all the characters are engaging, no matter how despicable they are. Not for the faint of heart, but this novel's character studies and ever shifting plot will excite fans of English noir." **Kirkus — a Recommended read.**

"*The Evil And The Pure* is a deliciously dark delight; a gritty, realistic look at the depths of human depravity. The twists and turns have you reeling with shock. A glory to read." **Matthew R Bell's BookBlogBonanza.**

"I found myself brilliantly horrified and captivated as I read and was taken along on a dark journey with a range of dangerous, sick and even innocent characters." **Chase That Horizon.**

"An amazing read. It's got the cast complexity of a Maeve Binchy novel as if written by a violent madman, and I mean that as a compliment!" **Kelly Smith Reviews.**

SUNBURN

"A well-written and disturbing piece of fiction. The plot reads like an international horror movie, enticing the reader with a series of detailed and comedic chapters before exploding into a vision of blood-chilling gore." **Books, Films & Random Lunacy.**

"This demonic masterpiece will not disappoint even the biggest of horror fans." **Crossing Pixies.**

"The elements of classic horror are very much present here. *Sunburn* held me firmly in the moment, demanding my full attention right to the very last page." **Thoughts Of An Overactive Imagination.**

"Like the *Hostel* films, they have a lot of set up and then shizzle hits the fan… and then hits it again for good measure!" **Dark Readers.**

Molls Like It Hot

by Darren Dash

Copyright © 2019 by Home Of The Damned Ltd

Cover design by Liam Fitzgerald. www.frequency.ie

Edited by Zoe Markham http://markhamcorrect.com

First electronic edition published by Home Of The Damned Ltd December 2019

First physical edition published by Home Of The Damned Ltd December 2019

The right of Darren Dash to be identified as the Author of the Work has been asserted by him in accordance with the Copyright, Designs and Patents Act 1988.

All rights reserved. No part of this publication may be reproduced, stored in a retrieval system, or transmitted, in any form or by any means without the prior written permission of the publisher, nor be otherwise circulated in any form of binding or cover other than that in which it is published and without a similar condition being imposed on the subsequent purchaser.

All characters in this publication are fictitious and any resemblance to real persons, living or dead is purely coincidental.

www.darrendashbooks.com

MOLLS LIKE IT HOT

DARREN DASH

HOME OF THE
DAMNED LTD

ONE — FIRST IMPRESSIONS

London was a city submerged. We'd endured one of the worst weeks of rain I'd ever experienced. Liquid pellets that could blind you, hurled to earth in an almost constant fury. Gutters everywhere were overflowing and the narrow, twisting backstreets looked more like the canals of Venice. The deluge had eased this evening but dark clouds still mobbed together thickly overhead like the backdrop to a movie about Vikings, threatening more mayhem. Anyone with any sense had settled in for the night in front of their television or tablet, smartphone in hand, safe in the shelter of their warm, dry pad.

I own an old-school TV, the kind that has actual depth, and I can access the internet on my phone if I really, really have to (the online translation services are a godsend when I get a passenger who can't speak English), but except for watching a couple of DVDs on my player every week, I rarely spend much time on either. The distraction that so many people find in them has always eluded me.

Work is my main way of putting the worries of the world to one side for those long, waking hours which can torment the troubled mind so wolfishly. The hours slip by sweetly when I'm on the streets in my cab, wending my way through the asphalt cobwebs of the city, hunting for fares and focusing on my routes. I tend not to think too much when I'm behind the wheel, and it's been a long time since deep thoughts were any friend of mine.

I'd picked up a couple of short rides within half an hour of clocking on, but not one in the three hours since. I'd known slow patches before but nothing like this. Deserted, flooded streets, nobody coming home early from a party, no hookers on their way to a hotel, no wayward tourists who'd taken a wrong turn on a self-guided Jack the Ripper walking tour, no shift workers eager to get home to a hot dinner and bed. I was starting to think I'd have to hit the West End. I hate it up there, way too congested for my liking. I almost never go touting for business around the perpetually thronged focal points of London, preferring the lonelier, lesser-known areas where a cabbie's knowledge of his runs can be properly tested. But the night was darkening and closing in around me. This place was dead.

Then the gunfire started.

I was a little east of Shoreditch, cruising down the middle of the road, no traffic coming against me, trying to avoid the moats on either side. I slowed when I heard the shots and cautiously scoped the scene. Nobody in sight. Any other night, I'd have floored the accelerator and got the hell out of Dodge. But I was bored. I had a headache from staring out at rain through my windshield for a week. I was annoyed at having gone so long without a fare. And maybe (just maybe) I didn't want to show fear. I can be dumb like that sometimes.

Whatever the reason, I pulled up where I was (nothing was going to persuade me to brave the floods by the kerb) and hung about to see what happened.

The gunfire buzzed closer. It sounded like several guns at first, blasting away in turn, but was down to two by the time a guy in filthy but flashy shoes burst out of an alleyway to my right, fell to his knees, turned and fired wildly into the shadows.

He was dressed smartly but his suit, like his shoes, was in a sorry state, spattered with dirty water and muck, a hole in the left arm where he'd been caught, blood oozing from it and staining the material of the jacket. He got to one foot and fired off a few more measured shots. I saw a couple of bullets strike the pavement near him, and one hit a window across the street, triggering an alarm. A more gullible man might assume that meant the police or security guards would swiftly be on the scene, but given the weather, I reckoned Jesus Christ was more likely to put in an appearance first, perched atop his cross and using it as a canoe.

The guy in the shoes stood, fired another two shots into the darkness, then relaxed his guard. Let his gun rest by his side. Wiped his forehead with a shaking hand and turned to see if there were any witnesses.

He saw *me*.

I turned off the FOR HIRE sign on my taxi and waited patiently. I watched the gun rise a little, then drop back into place. The guy wiped around his mouth with a sleeve, hitched up his trousers, examined his soiled, soaked shoes, shook his head glumly and went back into the alley. There was a shot a couple of seconds later, a pause, then one final retort. He re-emerged and waded through the floodwater to where I was poised, engine running.

I rolled down the window and studied him up-close. Brown hair, greying at the edges, a trim moustache. Thick around the middle, but he looked like he worked out regularly and had the fat under control. Expensive gear, especially the shoes. They looked like real snakeskin, studded with jewels across the toes and around the ankles. The gems glittered, even in the gloom and the rain.

"Need a ride?" I asked.

He looked at the gun in his hand, at the blood spreading from his wound, the alley, the floods, the car, finally at me.

He laughed, not in a kind way.

"Fucking mind reader we have here. Yes, I need a fucking ride."

He went to get in the back.

"No," I stopped him. "Not until you clean off."

"The fuck?" He squinted, gun rising again.

"You're covered in all kinds of shit," I said. "And you're bleeding. Brush off the worst of the dirt, dress your wound, then I'll let you in."

He looked down at his clothes again, then at his bleeding arm. "Are you fucking with me?" he snapped.

"I don't own the car," I explained. "I drive it nights but it belongs to a friend. If I take it back to him in the morning, seats ruined with filth and blood, how's he going to react?"

The guy stepped back and bent to peer into the cab. Gripped the lowered glass with his left hand. Pointed the gun at me with his right. "Friend," he hissed, "I don't know if you've noticed, but we've a situation on our hands. Two dead bodies in that alley, more in the streets behind. An alarm blaring. The police will swarm us any second now. I'm holding a gun that's hotter than hell. So quit acting the clown and –"

"We've got time," I interrupted, "*if* you hurry and don't stand there telling me things I already know."

The guy cocked his head. Held my gaze a long moment. I didn't flinch, just pointed at the meter, which was running. He smiled thinly, stepped back and shrugged off his jacket. I tossed him one of the plastic bags that I keep by my feet for cleaning up after my messier clients. He folded the jacket and stuck it in. Took off his shirt – he was wearing a white T-shirt beneath – and ripped it into strips. Cleaned around the wound in his arm as best he could. It looked like the bullet had passed through. A flesh wound. Lucky him. He wrapped it tight to stop the blood. Brushed down his trousers. Wiped his shoes. Offered himself for my approval and treated me to a sarcastic twirl.

"Do I pass muster?" he asked fake-sweetly.

"Good as gold," I said and let him in. As soon as the door shut, I moved off. Drove steadily, as if this was an average punter. I knew it was madness picking him up, but I didn't give a damn. With business as bad as it had been for the last week, a fare was a fare.

"You pick up shooters like me often?" the guy asked.

He'd settled in and got his breath back. I was heading further east, putting distance between us and the bodies. I hadn't waited for him to name a destination. He could do that later. For the time being I was calling the shots.

"You're lucky," I told him. "It's like a morgue out there tonight. You were the only fare I could find."

"You're very relaxed about this," he noted.

"You complaining?"

"No," he smiled. "It's just, most guys in your place would have sped up and drove on. *I* sure as hell wouldn't have stopped."

I shrugged. "Way I saw it, I'd stumbled into the middle of a street war. If I'd tried to take off, maybe you'd have panicked, pegged me as a witness who could testify against you, and shot me through the back of my head. But if I presented myself as a willing accomplice… well, you'd have to be crazy not to see me as the good thing that I am, accept the ride and tip damn well when I drop you off."

"I could just shoot you and dump the car," the guy said.

I shook my head. "Why complicate matters? I don't care who you are or what your business is. I'm not looking to extort you. I just want to be paid for the ride."

"How do you know I'll be that level-headed?" the guy challenged me.

"Survival of the fittest," I sniffed. "A showdown like that, the guy who walks away is the one with the steadiest nerves. He'll consider his options, make the right and reasoned call."

The guy mulled over my words as I ferried him ever further to safety, staring at me coldly, eyes narrowing. "You're awful worldly for a cabbie."

"You see everything there is to see when you drive around in one of these long enough," I replied.

He held up his gun and looked at me questioningly. I probably should have feigned ignorance, but that dumb part of me wanted to show off.

"A Walther P99."

He chuckled. "If it's good enough for the Germans, it's good enough for me. I haven't bothered with anything else in a long time."

"I'm Hi-Power all the way," I said.

He grunted. "Browning make a good handgun, there's no arguing with that. Popular with the Army boys."

I grunted back at him and said nothing more.

He lowered the gun and looked out at the rain, which was picking up again. "You got a name, friend?" he asked after a while. He could have just read it off my driver display card, but I guess he wanted to be sociable.

"Eyrie Brown."

The guy blinked. "*Eerie* as in ghosts and weird shit?"

"*Eyrie* as in where falcons nest," I corrected him. "Had an uncle who was a twitcher. He suggested it as a joke but it caught my mother's fancy."

"Eyrie Brown." The guy thought for a few seconds. "Doesn't ring any bells."

"No reason why it should. I'm just a cabbie."

"Oh really?"

I looked in the mirror. He was still facing the rain, but I knew he was seeing me regardless. Trying to see *into* me, finding it hard to believe my appearance at such a delicate moment could be a mere coincidence.

"Really," I said softly.

"Just luck you were in the right spot to pick me up tonight?"

"Just luck," I confirmed.

He gave it a long, dangerous few seconds, then sniffed. "I guess I got no other choice but to believe you. So, where you heading?"

"Right now I'm just driving, waiting for you to direct me."

He took a moment, eyes half closed, trying to map his way to a safe house. "South to Deptford. I don't want to go home. Might be some nasty surprises lying in store, know what I mean?"

"No. Don't want to, either."

"Because you're just a cabbie, right?" His eyes twinkled.

"Right." My eyes stayed flat.

"I'm Lewis Brue," he told me, leaning forward to shake hands while I was stopped for a red light. I think he expected a reaction but I hadn't heard of him. Didn't want to admit as much, so instead I asked if his arm was OK. He grimaced. "Hurts like a bitch, but the bullet passed through, so it should be easy to patch up. You ever take a bullet?"

"Always managed to avoid them."

"Lucky man." The light changed and I eased on. "So, Eyrie Brown," he said, "you always been a driver?"

"Been doing it for a couple of years now."

"What were you before?"

I thought about lying or ignoring the question, but I gave too much away when we were talking about guns. Like he said, all the Army boys love a Hi-Power.

"I was in the Forces." I kept it as vague as possible. The past a closed book for me, as the old saying goes.

"I figured," he smirked. "See any action?" I shot an irritated look his way and he winced. "Not the sort of question I'm supposed to ask, huh?"

"It was a long time ago," I said neutrally.

He took the hint and left it at that, which I appreciated.

I drove in silence for a time. He didn't like it when we hit a busy road, drew back into the shadows, so I stuck to the darker areas as best I could, which was fine by me, as I preferred the darkness too.

"You married?" he asked suddenly.

"No."

"Girlfriend?"

"Not right now."

"Kids?"

"You want to write my biography?"

"Just making small talk. I have a wife, but we separated years ago. Three kids. The oldest's nearly seventeen. Sharp as a scalpel. Wants to be a doctor."

"Good money."

He pulled a face. "Not as much as I make, but he's not cut out for a life like mine. The youngest – they're all boys – maybe he has a chance. Not sure if I want that for him or not, but I won't stand in his way if he sets his heart on it."

I didn't ask what Lewis Brue did for a living. Didn't really need to. I wasn't naïve.

"How old are you, Brown?" he asked. "Early thirties?"

"Thereabouts."

"If you don't mind a bit of advice from an older guy who's been there and done it, I'd suggest you crack on and sow your seed. Don't want to be too old to see the kids grow up. Didn't work out for me and the missus, but I'm glad I went into action when I did. I got to enjoy the boys. Might get to have fun with the grandkids too if I stay fit and keep dodging the bullets."

"We're getting close to Deptford," I said. "Want to start giving me directions?"

He looked over my shoulder. Clocked the name of the street. "Hang a right." He smiled ruefully at me. "Did you ask that just to shut me up about the kids?"

"Yes."

He laughed, not offended. "Fair enough. Your car."

"My friend's."

"Oh yeah." He scratched an ear. "Want me to buy it for you?"

I frowned. "I wasn't expecting *that* big a tip."

"Hey, you work for me, the sky's the limit."

The frown deepened. "Work for you?"

"Why not? I like your style, Eyrie Brown. I know next to nothing about you, but what does that matter? I'm all about first impressions. Come work for me. Whatever you're good at, we'll find somewhere for you to slot in."

I thought it over for a minute, to be polite. Then I shook my head. "Thanks for the offer but I like being a cabbie. Spent too long doing the Knowledge to just turn my back on it."

"That's a pity. I could do with more men like you. Left at the next lights."

I drove in silence again. He took out a cigarette and lit up. Normally I wouldn't let anyone smoke in the taxi – regardless of the fact that it's illegal, Dave hates the smell of smoke – but this one time I made an exception.

Lewis looked at his hand, which was still trembling a little, and snorted. "Want to know a funny thing? I was scared back there."

"That's understandable," I said.

"I mean really scared. When they started shooting, and I saw how many I was up against, I thought, *This is it, I'm a goner, they're gonna kill me.* My stomach went funny. I almost didn't get my gun out in time to return fire. I was never scared like that before. When I was younger, I got off on violence. Better than sex, in its own way. But tonight I only knew fear. I imagined my kids at my funeral, tears in their eyes, and... Am I boring you again?"

"A little."

He flipped me the finger, but he was chuckling. "You ever know fear like that, my friend?" he asked softly.

My thoughts snapped back to the desert. Zahra. Dancing James. The photos I stuck on the wall above the foot of my bed when I got my flat in London. Taking them down and burning them a few weeks later, not needing them, the faces always there in my head whenever I closed my eyes.

I didn't answer the question, just let it linger and worry us both.

Lewis Brue flexed the fingers of his injured arm and studied me some more in the mirror. The question about fear had come from a genuine place, but now he was looking crafty, probing for secrets of my own. "You ever kill anyone, Eyrie Brown?" he asked.

I didn't answer.

"Not my place to ask?" he murmured.

I flashed him a look. He nodded, sat back and gazed out into the dark, leaving me to focus on the road and drive.

We pulled up outside a two-storey house close to Deptford station. Completely dark downstairs, but a light was on in one of the rooms up top.

Brue leant forward and chewed a thumb, making no move to get out.

"Not sure this is safe?" I asked.

"Yeah," he breathed. "I trust this guy, but something like this puts questions in your mind. I remember him talking about wanting to get a new place last summer, somewhere with a pool.

Couldn't afford it. Maybe someone offered him the money he needed. Maybe they threw in enough for a diving board and all."

"Only one way to find out," I said.

"Yeah." Still he didn't move. "Maybe you could –"

"No," I said.

"What?" he snapped. "You don't know what I was gonna say."

"You were about to ask me to ring the bell and check if everything's OK."

"Fuck. You *can* read minds." He chewed the thumb some more. "I could make it worth your while."

"I'm sure you could," I told him. "And if you had a suitcase full of cash on you, I'd be tempted. But from what I've gathered, your long-term prospects don't look so hot, therefore your IOU doesn't interest me."

"Then you can be bought?" Lewis asked with a smile.

"To press a bell?" I echoed the smile. "Yes, if things were different, you could pay me to do that. I won't give up the day job, but only a fool turns down a nice little earner on the side."

"I'll bear that in mind," he grinned, then sighed and stared at the house. "Think I should risk it?"

I shrugged. "If you're lucky, he joined a gym with a members pool."

Brue snorted on a laugh.

"I'll take you somewhere else if you prefer," I said.

"But where?" he asked himself, then cocked an eyebrow at me. "I could come back to your place. No one knows about *you*. I'd surely be safe there."

I shook my head. "I'd rather not take my work home with me."

He choked back another laugh and picked up the bag with his jacket in it. "I know we only just met, but I like you a lot, Eyrie Brown. If you ever change your mind about the job…"

"I'll come looking for you," I promised, and I meant it, experienced enough to know that nobody can predict what the future might hold. "I don't think you'll be a hard man to find."

"Shouldn't be," he muttered. "I just hope you don't find me resting in a pine box six feet under."

He opened the door and stepped out into the rain. He put a hand into a pocket and pulled out his wallet. Ignoring the meter, he counted off a lot of twenties and held them out. "That enough for your troubles?"

"That'll do nicely," I said, taking the money.

"Thanks, Brown. You did me a good turn tonight. I won't forget it."

I half-nodded, pocketing the cash. "I hope it goes OK for you in there."

"Me too," he said drily, then shut the door and waded through the rain, shoulders hunched.

I didn't stay to watch him ring the bell. Reversing back the way I'd come, I took a left and headed west, looking for another fare, but it was almost an hour until the next one, and that was only a short ride, like the two at the start of my shift. Some nights you just can't catch a break, I mused as I clocked off and turned for home.

I touched the wad of twenties in my pocket and smiled.

But some nights you can.

TWO — THE GANG

"You're pathetic, the lot of you! Boxers? You couldn't punch your way out of a coronation chicken wrap! For *this* I get out of bed in the morning?"

Fervent Eld spat by his feet and mumbled some curses that the boys in the gym couldn't hear. None of the kids took any notice. Fervent was always ripping into them, so they knew he didn't mean it. They were his world, no matter their flaws, and he'd have stood up for every single one of them. Often had, taking the fight outside the gym to drunken, abusive fathers, or drug dealers looking to sink their claws into Eld's youthful charges. Sometimes he won those battles, more often he lost, but he always stood up for the boys.

Fervent flopped down beside me and rubbed his knees. He'd been complaining of aches ever since I'd met him, when I'd been a kid like those in the gym today. He'd been to every doctor and physio he could afford, acupuncturists and more, but none could do anything for him. The only relief came when one of his boys won a fight — then he was prancing around, delighted, pain temporarily forgotten. Sadly for Fervent, that didn't happen too often. He had all the enthusiasm and dedication of a puppy, but he was no mastermind of the ring. Not that he saw it that way. Fervent believed (most fervently, it must be said, to get the pun out of the way nice and early) with all his heart that the failures on fight night lay with the kids, not their coach.

"They're piss-poor, Eyrie," he said softly, close to tears, holding his hand in front of his face so the teenagers who were sparring and training couldn't see. "I swear, all my years, I've never seen a shower as bad as this lot."

"There must be a few who have what it takes," I protested, politely refraining from pointing out the number of times he'd spun this line before. Every generation seemed to throw up the worst shower of boxers that Fervent had ever seen.

"Yeah?" he snorted. "Name one. You've seen them all in action. Go on."

I was silent.

"There!" His eyes gleamed triumphantly, but the gleam swiftly faded as he realised how hollow his victory was. "I should retire," he groaned. "I'm too old, been here too long. I can't teach these guys. They need someone younger, with new ideas, fire in his belly. I'm an old warhorse."

Fervent had been threatening to quit for almost as long as he'd been trotting out clichés, but it had been getting worse these past four or five years, since his last young pretender had waltzed off in chase of fame and glory. Despite his protests to the contrary, Fervent had trained several good fighters over the years, when they were young and (to utilise a cliché as Fervent would) learning the ropes, but not one of the ungrateful little shits had ever taken him along for the ride when they progressed to bigger, better things. He was viewed by those in the know as a kids' trainer, reasonably useful at spotting talent and lining boys up for their first steps to relative glory, but not the man you needed to take a winner forward.

The sad truth was, those in the know were right. Still, they should have allowed him to tag along as a passenger at least once, so he could have experienced big nights as a member of a winning team. But boxing was a cruel world and none of the ring sharks who flourished in its bloodied waters cared about the ghosts of dedicated, inspirational but plodding Fervent Elds. They used these anonymous old men and discarded them, and the kids did the same when they were told to choose, because they knew where the money lay, and it didn't lie in sentimental loyalty.

I stood to watch some of the boys going through their paces. I came to Fervent's a lot. It wasn't actually called that. GINO'S was the name on the sign outside. But Fervent had been running the place as long as anyone could remember and everyone always referred to it as his.

The gym didn't distract me the way driving did, but it gave me interaction with people who weren't paying for the pleasure, and that was important. I needed to be a loner to survive, but I was aware that, if I didn't take care, I could be too much of a loner for my own good. As antisocial as I was, I did need a few friends to spend time with. Otherwise what was I surviving *for*?

I'd always loved the ring. Dreams of being a pro when I was younger. Fervent still maintained that I could have made the grade, a scrappy southpaw who had a knack for getting in behind the defences of better, stronger fighters. I'd trained here until the age of fifteen, when I went off the rails a bit, nothing too crazy, just normal teenage rebellion. Fervent used to chew me out. He thought I could be a winner and he always went tough on those he believed in. He tried everything to get me to train hard and push myself, but I saw him as a crazy old man and didn't listen. That still caused me to blush with shame sometimes.

I picked up the gloves again in the Army, but I'd been away from the ring too long by that stage. A handy amateur, nothing more. I still occasionally dreamt about fighting in Vegas, Caesar's

Palace, the main attraction. I hope I never grow out of those childish dreams entirely. Even old men on their deathbed should have dreams. Zahra used to say that.

A hard lump formed in my throat, the way it still did whenever I thought of her name, even all these years later. Trying to push her from my thoughts – I preferred to think about her late at night, when I was alone and unable to sleep – I focused on the young boxers and tried to select a potential champion.

"What about Cat?" I asked, nodding at a lean welterweight.

"A cut above most," Fervent grudgingly admitted, "but he's been missing training, hanging with the wrong crowd. Chasing girls, but the ones he's chasing are the ones he should run from. He has potential but he's wasting it."

"Barney?" I tried. A sturdy middleweight, a southpaw like me.

"Can't take a punch. Strong as Samson. Be a good arm-wrestler, but won't make it in the ring. I tell you, not one of them will amount to anything. It tears me up to say it, but it's the truth. We're a laughing stock. Everyone wants to take us on, to score a few easy wins and boost morale. We're a fucking joke."

I sat and took a slug of water. I'd have preferred a beer but Fervent had long ago outlawed alcohol in the gym. "So there's no point me putting any money in?" I asked.

"Be a waste of time," he sighed, and I knew the honesty hurt. Fervent always needed a bit of extra cash to keep afloat. He wouldn't have turned me down unless he genuinely felt it would be wrong to take my money.

I'd been looking to invest in a boxer for a while. I didn't have a huge amount put aside, but I was working long hours and banking a nice chunk every week (when the city wasn't flooding), and I had few overheads or leisure buys. When someone from my bank had phoned and asked me if I wanted to move my savings out of my current account and do something more with the money, I'd figured it was time to look for a way to spend it. I knew and cared nothing about the stock market, and property didn't interest me either. Having thought about it for a few weeks, I decided to find a young boxer with skill and stamina, sink my earnings into his training, go along with him as far as I could, make a tidy profit, maybe do it again a few times, until I had enough to buy a place like Fervent's and go into business if I ever tired of the cab.

Fervent coughed and pointed to a tall black guy, one of the oldest trainees. "Berry. Twenty-two. Should have quit two or three years ago, but still thinks he can be a star, begging me to help him push on." He paused and tugged at his lower lip. "I'm thinking of putting him into bare-knuckle fights. What do you reckon?"

I shrugged. "He's tough. A brawler. He'd do OK."

"I hate having to tell them," Fervent said. "Nothing worse than hearing you're finished with the gloves. But it suits some guys, if they want to make money and still feel the hunger to fight."

"Yeah," I said softly. "I know."

I'd come out of the Army directionless and penniless. To earn some cash, I'd gone back to Fervent's, started training again, thinking I might make enough in the ring to get by. He'd given me a month, then told me I was too old, my chance had passed, and there was more money to be made if I went bare.

I'd known about those events but always assumed they were for Gypsies and Eastern Europeans. Never thought I might end up in a dark gym, late at night, no gloves, bloodthirsty vultures crowded close as they could get, orgasmic grins, cash exchanging hands all the time, flying through the air like confetti at a wedding (before it was banned). Punching until one of you could no longer stand. Having to guard against bites, low blows, the occasional karate kick. Rules made and broken night-by-night. Fervent always in my corner, encouraging and sustaining me, telling me it was only for a short time, just to make enough money to get me out of a hole and set me on the straight and narrow.

Depressing, despairing work, but I made more in those fights than I ever did at anything else. I'd have carried on earning if I'd kept going, but I retired early, the night I saw a Lithuanian poke a Pole's eye out, and the poor one-eyed bastard still boxed on, because that was all there was to his life. I got out of the game the next day, roughed it for a time, before Dave asked if I'd ever thought about trying the Knowledge and becoming a cabbie.

"If Berry wants to discuss it with someone who's been there, I'm happy to talk with him," I said.

Fervent smiled guiltily. "I was hoping you'd say that."

"Hoping I'll put him off with my tales?" I guessed.

Fervent shrugged. "I'll back him if he goes down that path, but I like to give my guys as many of the facts as I can before they commit. A lot of them don't think about all the bad shit that can happen, only the good."

I hung around a while longer, helped out where I could, let the boys rile me, taking their baits with good humour, knowing there was nothing malicious in them. I'd been the same at that age, gobby, thinking I was smarter and funnier than I was.

I caught up with Fervent again just before I left. "Keep looking for me," I told him. "If you find a contender, I'll cut you in like I promised, keep you in the game as long as I can."

"Consider it a deal," Fervent chuckled as he shook my hand, his crooked fingers bent with arthritis, every bit of him bent except his eyes, which were full of hope, no matter what he might have been saying a short while ago. Those eyes were back on his boys before I turned to leave. His gaze rarely left them for long. They might be the worst bunch he'd ever trained (since the last worst bunch) but they were still his kids and he cared for them like the fathers so many of them had never known.

TERRY'S. One of my favourite cafés. The food was affordable, came in decent portions, and only rarely poisoned you. Fine music on the jukebox, lots of early rock greats like the Stones, the Who, the Kinks.

I hung out at TERRY'S most evenings before clocking on. It was where I met Dave and borrowed the keys to his cab. Occasionally I picked it up from the garage where he parked it when not in use – that's where I dropped it off at the end of my shift each night, leaving the keys with whoever was on duty – but more often than not we met in TERRY'S. Dave drove days. He'd done nights as well once, working fifteen or sixteen-hour shifts, before he fell in love and got married. Now he liked to spend his nights at home. Even took the odd day or two off, when the wife wanted to go to a show or a fancy restaurant.

"Have a bite of my burger," No Nose said to Mickey Goodnews.

"Fuck off," Goodnews bit back.

"Go on, it'll do you good. Just one bite. Do it for No Nose. Come on, open wide, open wide." No Nose tried forcing the bun into Mickey's mouth, but he was only playing and was easily turned aside by the indignant Irishman. (In fact they both had Irish backgrounds, but Goodnews played it up more.)

"Fecking savages," Goodnews sneered. He was vegetarian. Had been since the family dog choked to death on a chicken bone.

"Don't know what you're missing, Mick." No Nose licked his lips and bit into the burger. They didn't do especially good burgers at TERRY'S but you wouldn't have guessed that from No Nose's rapturous expression.

We'd all passed the Knowledge, but No Nose was the most street savvy cabbie I'd ever met. He knew about routes that the rest of us never even guessed existed. He loved driving and cruised the streets in his spare time, watching London go about its continual evolution, studying buildings and neighbourhoods as they rose and fell and rose again over the years.

"Lucy, tell Mickey what he's missing," No Nose said to the small woman to his left. Lucy just smiled. She hardly ever spoke. She was shy, even around friends. A capable but cautious driver. Always put safety first, and anticipated danger as if she had a sixth sense for it. The only one of us never to have had a crash, even though she'd been at it longer than me, longer than Dave, almost as long as Mickey Goodnews. She was a pretty, ginger lady. Had a crush on No Nose, despite the fact that he had a button of a nose that looked ludicrous in his broad, heavy face, but nothing had ever happened between them, at least not that any of us knew about.

"Don't listen to them, Goodnews," Adrian said. "That stuff's poison. The government put chemicals in it to stunt people's minds."

"It stunted your mind, that's for sure," Caspar giggled.

Adrian scowled, then nodded at Caspar. "Case in point. He eats steak tartare for breakfast and wonders why he ends up looking the way he does."

"What's wrong with the way I look?" Caspar growled.

"Check the mirror."

It was true. Caspar – who hated being called that – was as pale as the ghost he was named after, but far blotchier than any character you'd ever find on a kids' TV show. His puckered, marked face was like a map of some long lost islands out beyond Tahiti way.

A waiter refilled our cups. "Hey, Bernárd," Mickey Goodnews said. "You cook, right? You studied to be a chef?"

"I did," Bernárd said. "Still hope to run a kitchen one day."

"Then you know about these things. Tell them. Meat is poison, yeah? Full of chemicals that cause cancer and brain damage, right?"

"Sorry," Bernárd smiled. "Not my place to put the customers off their food. All I can say is that my grandmother ate meat at every meal, all her life, and she lived to be ninety-three, never lost her senses, and only died when she was run over by a bus on her way to play a game of tennis." He moved away to serve a table of truckers.

"A game of tennis," I chuckled. "He should be on stage. Caspar, pass the sugar."

"It's Charles," he snapped, shoving the mug filled with sugar cubes my way. "Not Caspar. You know I hate that name. Why do you always –"

"Shut up already, you tart," Dave shouted, entering the café, slapping Caspar over the head as he moved to take his seat. "I come in from a hard day's work, this is what I have to listen to? Behave."

"Up yours," Caspar grunted but he couldn't help smiling. Everyone liked Dave, one of those guys you naturally warmed to.

"You're talking about meat again, aren't you?" Dave guessed. "The same old argument. Don't you ever get tired of rattling on? Hey, Bernárd, a coffee please, quick as you can before I die of thirst."

"Coming up," the waiter called back.

"Any news?" Dave asked.

"Yeah," Goodnews beamed. "You'll never guess who Eyrie picked up last week while the rest of us were sheltering from the storm."

I groaned, regretting ever bringing it up. Lewis Brue was much better known than I'd anticipated. My interesting story, which I thought would be a conversation piece for a few minutes, was a major saga as far as the others were concerned.

I'd already gone through the tale three times, but Dave looked at me with open curiosity and an eager smile, and I didn't have the heart to disappoint him.

"I was east of Shoreditch and hadn't had a fare for about three hours," I began, and out it all reeled again.

"I'll take two, no... three, no... hold on a minute, let me... two. Gimme two."

"You're sure?"

"No."

We all laughed. Mickey Goodnews was a lousy gambler. No Nose flicked a chip at him and told him to get on with it and make up his mind. Goodnews reacted with a curse. Then he sighed and asked Adrian to give him three cards. Lucy smiled at Goodnews sympathetically, then asked for a single card. Dave sat pat. And it was up to me to bet.

I should have been out earning my keep, but we'd started fooling with the cards in TERRY'S, then No Nose had produced a crate of craft beer – he had a cousin who worked in a supermarket and was always getting stuff cheap – and we'd got to bullshitting. Dave rang home and said he was working late, I decided to take the night off, and we ended up back at Caspar's for a late game.

"See your twenty. Raise you fifty." Adrian looked around the table and grinned. "Heat's on," he drawled. "Can you take it? I know Goodnews can't. I can see him folding already. Ain't that right, Mick?"

"Feck you," Mickey snapped and tossed in a couple of pound coins. "See you and raise." Then he winced and scratched the back of his neck, wondering if he'd done the right thing, wishing he could take back the money.

We never played for much. Kept it friendly. Never fleeced Mickey Goodnews, though we were about the only ones in the city who didn't. He couldn't play for shit but he loved to gamble. He'd sit in on a game for hours, or spend an entire day at the races, leave with empty pockets and still return the next day, believing this time he'd win, that his luck would turn eventually. We tried keeping an eye on him, to stop him slipping too far into debt – he already owed more than he could easily pay back – but he was a grown man, we had our own lives, and we couldn't watch out for him every hour of the day.

"See. Raise a pound." Lucy squinted apologetically at Goodnews. He shrugged and tried to make little of it, but you could see he'd fold as soon as the bet came back to him. Lucy was a shrewd player. Rumour had it she'd made a living at it once, before coming to London. She could make her face go blank as a mask. Always cool and in command. She was way too good for the likes of us, but played beneath her best, so we stood a chance. Not that she ever went away from one of our games with less than she'd started with.

"That was a decent little story you spun earlier," No Nose murmured as he studied his cards seriously through the old-fashioned spectacles he only ever wore when we were betting.

"I didn't know he was a big deal," I muttered, wanting the attention to pass.

"Lewis Brue?" No Nose tutted. "As Fervent Eld would no doubt put it, he's a major player. Surprised you'd never heard of him."

I shrugged. "I don't move in those circles. No interest in them."

"Even so," No Nose said, and raised another pound.

"Doesn't matter who it was," Dave grunted. "You shouldn't have let a killer in my cab, especially one who was bleeding like a stuck pig."

"It was only a trickle."

Dave grunted again. "And if others had shot at him while he was with you? If they'd shot up my car?"

"There was no one left to shoot. He'd killed them all."

"Oh well, that puts me right at ease." He shook his head. "It was a stupid move, Lyric. You don't want to go mixing with people like that."

"I know," I said quietly.

"So why do it?" he pressed.

I thought about Zahra and Dancing James.

"I hadn't had a fare in hours," I said. "I was bored."

Knowing that wasn't the truth. I hadn't known it that night. It had taken a few days of harsh introspection to figure it out and realise I'd been attracted to the danger, that I'd hoped for action, that part of me had wanted to get caught in crossfire or betrayed by the guy in the fancy shoes with the gun. Part of me had wanted to die, to escape the memories that had haunted me since the desert.

Maybe Dave saw through my lie. Maybe he guessed something of what I was thinking, even though I'd never told any of them about my past, the desert, Zahra and Dancing James. Maybe he just saw my pain and didn't want to cause any more. But whatever he knew or guessed, he let me be.

No Nose moved his glasses to the end of his nose (an almost minimal movement). "I ever tell you about the time Bond Gardiner sat in the back of my cab?" he asked and we all shook our heads and perked up. Every cabbie in the city has stories, but few can match No Nose's.

"I've been keeping it back for an occasion like this," No Nose said, "so that when someone came up with a really juicy story, I could top it."

"Why would you care about topping someone else's story?" Goodnews frowned.

"I'm known for my stories," No Nose said immodestly. "Don't like to blow all the big ones cheaply. I save them for the right time. Storytelling is all about the timing. Anyway, I was driving along one night – up round Tottenham, near as I can remember, though I've no idea why I would have been in such a backwater – and a couple of guys hail me. I stop and let them in. They sit in back. One of them tells me to drive. I forget where they wanted to go.

"After a while I look in the mirror, because they haven't said a word since they told me to drive. And it's a dangerous silence. Tension in the air, thick as a properly cut sandwich. So I look to see what's going on. And it's Bond Gardiner and some other guy."

"Who's Bond Gardiner?" Caspar asked. Then, as Lucy dealt, he added, "One."

"I'll take two," No Nose said, re-settling his glasses to examine his cards. "You remember Mikis Menderes? The Turk? One of London's bigger crime bosses a few years back?"

"I've heard of him."

"Well, Gardiner used to be his Tonto."

"He's an Indian — sorry, a Native American?"

We all laughed. "Shut the fuck up," Dave said kindly, "and let the man get on with his story. I'm out, by the way."

"Well, Bond Gardiner," No Nose continued, "is a mean-looking son of a bitch. I've had some hard screws in my car over the years, and he's up there with the hardest. The guy beside him, he's no prawn, but he looks tiny in comparison. And he's miserable as hell. On the point of crying, shaking and looking down at his shoes, saying nothing.

"This goes on, neither of them moving or saying anything, until Gardiner puts an arm across, slow as a sloth, sticks his right hand on top of the other guy's head and clamps him." No Nose put his cards down, spread his fingers and demonstrated for us. Picked up the cards and continued. "I'll bet a quid. The guy gives a little shriek. Makes like he's going to fight, then thinks twice and sags.

"Next, I see something shining and I try looking away, because I don't want to see this, not if it's going to be what I think it is, but I can't help myself. I'm fascinated because there's still no sound. So I keep checking, sneaky glimpses in the mirror, like Lot's wife, compelled to turn and stare.

"Gardiner, he — you're seeing me? Bollocks. I'm out. Someone throw me another beer." There was a pause while he opened the can. "Gardiner's got a thin blade. Lovely handle, ebony or something like that. He holds it in his left hand, puts the tip to the side of the other guy's head, holds him steady, and starts working it in."

Lucy shuffled the cards and dealt swiftly, faster than normal because she was concentrating on the story. We all were. She could have dealt herself four aces and no one would have noticed.

"The guy starts convulsing. Slaps Gardiner and tries to pull free, but Gardiner's too strong. He holds him there and the guy can't do anything. Gardiner keeps pushing it in, and the guy's mouth is open and he's dying and he's still not saying a word. And I'm watching, shitting myself because I'm a witness, but knowing there's nothing I can do to stop it.

"Then the blade catches on something. Gardiner gives it a shove but nothing happens. It's stuck, and the guy's not dead yet, so he grunts and pushes hard, and the knife snaps forwards at an angle and pops out through the guy's right eye, and the eyeball goes with it, slips off the blade and falls down his cheek."

"Christ," Mickey Goodnews gasped.

"Aye, aye," Adrian grinned.

"And I start laughing," No Nose said.

"*What*?" Caspar howled.

"I couldn't help it," No Nose said. "This poor guy, he's dying on my back seat, and his eye's dangling down his face, and I start laughing like I haven't since I saw Peter Kaye do a live gig way back when. It wasn't funny. I don't get off on violence. But what can I say? You had to be there."

"No thanks," Dave grunted.

"So — Jesus, Lucy, what sort of cards are these? Fuck it, I'll take three. So I'm laughing myself sick. And this guy's being murdered. And Bond Gardiner, mean son of a bitch, looks at me, amazed and pissed, like he can't believe it, like I'm the one behaving badly.

"Then he starts laughing too. He pulls the blade back, then pokes it through a bit more, and it pops out the other side of the guy's head, and he takes his hand away and leaves the blade there, like one of those fake knives you get in magic shops, and we howl even harder, and he taps the handle and it quivers up and down, and I had to pull over, I was crying with laughter."

"You sick fuck," Adrian said, shaking his head.

No Nose ignored the interruption and pressed on with the story.

"So there we are, pulled up, laughing ourselves stupid, a corpse in the car with us. Thank God there were no cops about.

Mind you, him being Bond Gardiner, they maybe wouldn't have bothered us anyway.

"After a few minutes Gardiner opens the door and gets out. Checks the meter and pays the exact fare, nothing extra. He sees I'm surprised that he's not tipping me – yeah, even with everything else that was happening, I was thinking about my tip, which is how you know I'm a real cabbie – and he smiles and says softly, 'Your life. That's what I'm giving you on top of the fare.' And he walks away and leaves me with the stiff. I look at the money. I look at the dead guy. And, God damn me, I started laughing again and didn't stop till I got home into bed and fell asleep."

No Nose chuckled at the memory, showed us his flush and raked in the chips to a chorus of groans and curses.

"Unbefuckinglievable," Caspar winced. "The one good hand I get all night and you top it. You two have a deal going?"

Lucy smiled and No Nose gave her a friendly hug.

"What happened to the body?" I asked.

"The body?" No Nose echoed.

"The corpse. What did you do with him?"

"Oh, yeah. I took him to a lonely spot near Margate and dumped him in the sea. Luckily there wasn't too much blood on the back seat, easy enough to clean. Got a fare on the way back and they never even noticed. I was gonna take the knife – Gardiner left it in his head – and keep it as a souvenir to remember the night by, but that would have been ghoulish."

"You dumped him?" Mickey Goodnews asked, amazed. "Wasn't that kind of… I mean, if I was killed like that, I'd want a proper funeral."

"Bollocks to that," No Nose snorted. "Was I supposed to

take him to the Old Bill, explain how he got there, dish the dirt on Bond Gardiner? You think I'm as dumb as I look?"

"I didn't realise you were such a cool customer," Adrian said.

"Yeah, well," No Nose said, sharing a short look with me that let me know he hadn't laughed too much about it in the years since, "when the shit hits the fan you deal with it or go have a breakdown. Now, where are my cards? I didn't come here to regale you buggers all night with my scintillating stories. I came here to play."

Everyone had gone except for Adrian and me. Caspar was there too, of course, it being his place, but he'd crashed a couple of hours back. Adrian fetched another beer from the fridge and we bet on highest card drawn. Fifty pence a time. Passing away the last few minutes until dawn, enjoying the peace and quiet.

"Ever play strip poker with Lucy?" Adrian asked.

"No. Damn — a three. That's the fourth low card I've had in six draws."

"The luck of the Irish."

"You're not Irish."

"I'm evidently more Irish than you. King. Top that."

"Six. This is getting ridiculous. So, did you get her naked?"

"Lucy? Nah. She tore us to pieces. Me, Dave and a few more. There were a couple of other girls there, we got to see some of their flesh, but not her."

"Surprised to hear that Dave was up for that."

Adrian grinned. "His wife was away. He'd had too much to drink. Didn't get up to any mischief, though we convinced him for a while in the morning that he had."

"When was this?"

"A few weeks back. We tried to ring you, but you were — shit, a deuce. Maybe your luck is changing."

We went on drawing.

"You were on a bender," Adrian said.

"A few weeks ago?" I shook my head. "I haven't been drunk for months."

"Oh?" He shrugged. "Must have been further back then."

I drink sensibly most of the time, beers with my friends, the occasional shot of rum to help me sleep. But every so often shit builds up inside my head and I have to release it. Happens maybe once or twice a year. I stack the kitchen with beer, rum, gin, some mixers, and hole up. Go wild for a week, open myself to the past, lose myself in the desert again, weep, scream, mourn. Come out of it shaken but here, suicide dodged, able to dream once again about a future where I don't have to do this, where I'm at ease with my past, not necessarily living pretty, but in a place where the demons can't find me.

My friends didn't seem to worry about my benders. Just part of who I was. They rarely passed comment, and if they had any inkling of how close to the cliff edge I sometimes came, they kept it to themselves.

I cut the cards a few more times, then sighed and leant back.

"You're done?" Adrian asked, surprised.

"A man's gotta sleep," I yawned.

"I suppose." He rose and stretched. "I'll come with you. We can share a ride and split the fare."

"Are we taking the drinks or leaving them?"

"Leave them for Caspar, so he knows that we appreciate him

letting us come play. Order a cab, let me have a slash, and we'll be going."

I used an app on my phone to call a car – one of the precious few apps that I'd ever downloaded – then drew again while I was waiting for Adrian, just to see what I'd reveal. A fucking three! Sometimes the universe comes straight out and tells you — time to throw in your cards and quit.

THREE — THE PROPOSITION

The weather was back to normal and so was business. Good runs every night, working past dawn most days. Busy and distracted, the way I liked it. Didn't see too much of the gang, or get to Fervent's as often as usual, but that's the way it goes sometimes. Only a fool voluntarily breaks an active streak. One of the first things Dave taught me.

A shower was the only thing on my mind as I hauled myself up the steps to my third-floor flat after another full-on shift. The rainstorms were a distant memory and London was sweltering. I was sweating fit to drown, even though it wasn't yet nine. I'd dropped the cab and keys off at the garage for Dave to collect later and made my way home — a brisk twenty-five minutes' stroll. A cool shower, a cold drink, then bed.

I saw the lock had been forced before I reached out to open it. I scowled and cursed beneath my breath. This was the third time in two years. I enjoyed living in Bermondsey, the flat was perfect for me, and the rent was reasonable as central London rates went, but maybe it was time to up stakes. I don't have much, so last time, along with the DVD player and my collection of DVDs, plus a few other bits and pieces that wouldn't make much of a profit, the thieves took all my bed sheets and towels, purely out of spite. (They didn't touch the TV. I guess they were worried their backs wouldn't stand the strain carrying it down the stairs.) This time they'd probably taken the shampoo and toothpaste as well. As long as they'd left my damn toothbrush...

I pushed open the door and entered. Looking to see what was missing. In a foul mood. Prepared for the worst.

But nothing was gone.

Instead a stranger was lying on my bed, whistling softly. Sat up when he saw me, bum-shuffled to the end of the bed and stood. Grinned nonchalantly and tugged at some folds in his suit, trying to tweak out the creases.

"You Eyrie Brown?" he asked.

"No," I said, pleasantly as you please. "You've got the wrong flat. Eyrie Brown lives in 3D. This is 3B."

"3B?" He frowned. "But that's where I was told to come. Eyrie Brown, 3B."

"No," I smiled. "You're wrong."

"This isn't 3B?"

"This *is* 3B, but Eyrie Brown's in 3D. Easy mistake, mixing up a B for a D. You're not the first."

I kept on smiling while he stared, but it was a forced smile. I hadn't a clue who he was or what he wanted, but I knew he wasn't here to deliver the milk.

"I think you *are* Eyrie Brown," he growled.

"I'm telling you, Eyrie Brown's 3C. Go along and –"

"3C?" He laughed. "You said 3D a second ago."

Shit. It had been a long night.

"OK," I sighed and sat on the chair beside the wall, letting my head rest against the plasterboard. "What do you want?"

"We're going for a drive," he said.

"You got anywhere special in mind?"

"Never mind what I've got in mind. You'll see when we get there."

"What's this about?" I asked.

He tapped his nose.

"If I don't come peacefully?" I said softly, wondering if he was armed and if I could get to a knife before he could draw.

He shrugged. "I won't force you."

"You won't?" That wasn't the answer I'd expected.

"This is an invitation, not a demand."

I sat there blinking, not sure what to make of that. Then I figured it would be easier to play along than try to make sense of it. "How about I have a shower before we go? I stink."

"I noticed," he said, nose wrinkling. "Go ahead, we're not in any rush."

Again, not what I'd anticipated. If this was a kidnapping, it was the weirdest damn kidnapping I'd ever heard of.

I shuffled to the bathroom, disrobed and got under the shower. Stayed in there a good ten minutes, the water lukewarm, letting it hit my head and flow down my back.

I felt fresher when I came out and pulled on clean clothes, but I was still none the wiser. The guy in the rumpled suit was standing by the window, staring out at the humble view. I considered asking him again what this was about, but I was sure he wouldn't tell me.

"I'm ready," I said.

"Follow me," he grunted and headed for the stairs.

I swung the door shut after me as I left and hoped no enterprising little gits would notice the busted lock and clean out the flat while I was away.

We drove in silence for more than forty minutes. I didn't even ask the guy's name. If I hadn't been so tired, or if he'd been more aggressive, maybe I'd have been more concerned, but as things were, I was content to lie back, stare out the window and half-doze.

We stopped outside a bookies. The driver parked in front of the doors and killed the engine. "Sit tight a minute," he said, stepping out. Went inside and returned with a spotty teenager in tow. Tossed him the keys, beckoned me and led the way around back.

We were somewhere north of the river but I wasn't sure where exactly. Hadn't bothered to pay attention.

The guy opened a door and led the way up a dark flight of stairs. I followed, feeling slightly apprehensive now that I was here, but curious more than anything else. I'd never been summoned to a secret meeting before. I was intrigued.

We got to the top of the stairs and my guide said, "Wait here."

He walked down a corridor and disappeared into a room at the end. He was back in less than a minute. "In you go."

I started forward but he didn't follow. "Aren't you coming?" I asked.

"No," he said, treating me to a faux saintly smile. "My work here is done."

I slouched to the end of the corridor – I felt hot and sweaty again – and entered the room. There was a large desk, but the man who was waiting for me was sitting in front of it, in one of two chairs which had been set facing each other. It took me several seconds to make him. It had been a few weeks and he looked different in the light, without a gun in his hand or muddied, bloodied clothes. In the end the diamonds on his shoes clued me in before my brain could put a name to the face.

"You remember me," he said when he saw a flicker of recognition in my eyes.

"Lewis Brue," I nodded, cagily sitting down.

"Didn't think you'd forget," he chuckled. "Can I get you something to drink?"

"A cold beer would be great."

"Give me a minute."

Brue got up and left the room. I closed my eyes while he was gone and waited in the quiet. Opened them when I heard him returning. Thanked him for the beer and downed a mouthful while he took his seat. He'd brought a tumbler of Jack Daniels for himself. Toasted me as he sipped.

"Rabbit give you any grief?" he asked.

The question made no sense to me, so I said, "Pardon?"

"Rabbit," he said again. "Was it all OK when he picked you up?"

I stared at Lewis Brue blankly, then put two and two together.

"Rabbit's the driver's name?"

"Yeah." Brue squinted at me. "Didn't you ask?"

"No."

He looked puzzled. "If a stranger turned up at *my* place, that's the first thing I'd want to know."

I shrugged.

"Was Rabbit polite when he asked you to come?" Brue pressed.

"Yes. He told me it was an invitation, not a demand."

"Good. You never know if people are going to do what you tell them. Rabbit's better at taking orders than most, but a lot of guys would have acted the thug, no matter what they'd been told. I'm glad you didn't feel forced to come."

"He did break the lock on my front door," I noted.

"Invoice me for the repair," Brue replied. "I mean that. I don't want to put you out of pocket."

There was a silence. I looked round the room. Drab, faded wallpaper, a touch of rising damp. Not much in the way of accessories. Hardly the sort of place I'd imagined a man like Brue operating out of.

"This your office?" I asked.

"No." He looked offended. "Just some hole I borrowed for a few hours. I want to keep our business private. Rabbit is the only one who knows about us."

"Business? Us?" We were getting straight down to it, which I appreciated. I was too exhausted for small talk.

Brue shifted forward on his chair. "You said you didn't want to come work for me, and that's fine, but you did me a favour and I'd like to return it."

"You paid me for the ride," I reminded him.

He sniffed. "That doesn't cover it. Took me a while to realise how lucky I got that night. Not many drivers would have picked me up. That was some impressive shit, and once I'd calmed down and reflected, I knew you deserved more than a handful of twenties."

I said nothing to that. I'd been more than happy with my take, but if he wanted to give me more, who was I to argue?

"I've done some checking on you," Brue continued. "The way you acted, I thought you must be more than just a cabbie, that you must have connections."

"I don't."

"So I discovered. I guess they trained you well in the Army."

I regarded him warily. "You found out about that?"

He cocked his head. "Didn't need to. You told me in the cab."

I had to think back. We were talking about guns. I let it slip.

"So why am I here, Mr Brue?" I asked.

He smiled. "I've something that might be of interest to you. A job."

I frowned. "I told you I wasn't interested. You just said as much. Why drag me in to make me an offer you know I won't accept?"

"Because I think you will." He made a fist of his right hand and jabbed the air with it. "You boxed when you were younger and you're looking to buy in as a trainer and promoter now, right?"

My eyes narrowed. "You've been talking to Fervent Eld."

"Not personally, but he was approached. A nice old guy by the sound of things. Thinks very highly of you. Discussed your relationship openly, no reason why he shouldn't. He said you've got some money banked, just waiting for a kid with promise to come along."

I nodded, but I was still wary. "Why are you interested in my dealings with Fervent Eld? Are you looking to become a silent partner?"

Lewis Brue snorted. "Boxing was never my thing, but I'd like to see you do well, and I think I can help you out. I'm guessing you don't have a huge amount set by. Enough to train up a local boy who shows some spark, but not enough to go out and headhunt genuine talent. If you help me with a little problem, a one-off job, I'll put twenty-five K straight into your hand."

My eyes widened with genuine surprise.

"You can say no if you want," he said. "I won't harass you. If you want to take the job, great. If you don't, I'll hire someone else. I've come to you because I'd like to see us properly squared, but if you're uncomfortable with what I propose, I'll find another way to pay you back."

"Twenty-five thousand..." I said softly.

"You could do a lot with money like that," Brue noted. "Search for a quality fighter. Buy some decent equipment for Eld's place. Set up fights with established names when he's ready. I don't know much about boxing but I'm pretty sure it's a world where everything runs a whole lot smoother if you have extra cash to splash around."

"What would I have to do?" I asked quietly. I had no wish to tie myself to a man like Lewis Brue, but twenty-five thousand pounds was a lot of money to a man like me. Only a fool would turn it down without checking to see what strings were attached.

"You're interested?" he countered.

"If I don't have to do anything too incriminating... maybe."

"You understand how these things work?" he pressed. "If you listen, and you don't like what I have to say, then you *haven't* listened. Not a word of this makes it beyond these walls. You can leave now if you want, and tell your friends about the crazy gangster who made you a crazy offer, and I won't blink. But if you stay, you owe me your silence. You'll still be able to say no to the deal, but you never talk about it with anyone else. Are we clear?"

I tossed back half the bottle of beer.

I thought it over.

I nodded.

*

"There's a girl. *Toni*. I want her guarded for a few days."

"How old?"

"Early twenties."

"Who is she?"

"That's not for you to know."

"How long would it be?"

"This is Thursday morning." I almost sarcastically thanked him for reminding me of that, but this wasn't the time for levity. "If you accept the job, you can go home, catch some sleep, get up in the evening as normal. But instead of going out to work tonight, stay in. Toni will come to you around eight or nine. Babysit her through the weekend. I'll want her back here Sunday evening at five."

I stared into my bottle of beer and considered the proposal.

"Is it dangerous?" I asked.

"Shouldn't be."

"Don't lie to me."

"Who's lying?"

"Twenty-five thousand says this is no normal babysitting job. If trouble's part of the package, if my life's going to be in danger, I need to know."

He sniffed. "She has enemies but they won't know she's in London. If they find out, they don't know you, so they won't know where to look for her, unless they happen to spot you together on the move. I don't expect them to find out that she's here, and even if they do, I'd be shocked if you cross paths with them. You don't move in the same circles. You're not part of their world. It should be easy money."

"But if they *do* see me with her and find out where I live?" I pressed.

He shrugged. "Then they'll come for her and they'll come hard. You'll have to fight or flee."

"Will they come with guns?"

"I'd imagine so."

"A couple of guys? Dozens?"

"Not dozens. Maybe a few. They'll be able to handle themselves, but knowing what I know about your background, I understand that you can handle yourself too. I wouldn't be talking to you if I didn't think you were their equal."

"How hard would they fight for her? What would I have to do to make them lose interest? Break a few bones? Kill them?"

Brue looked away. "In a worst case scenario it'd be you or them, kill or be killed." Fervent Eld would have admired the clichés. "But if that happens and your hand is forced, it's worth bearing in mind that these people aren't strangers to the game. You wouldn't be killing anyone who doesn't deserve it."

I didn't like that. I could take care of myself in a fight, and I wasn't frightened by the prospect of violence or death. But this wasn't my scene. I'd never gone looking for trouble since I parted company with the Army.

But twenty-five thousand…

"Why not use one of your own men?" I asked. "You've never seen me in action. I wasn't in any danger that night when I picked you up. I didn't have to fight. How do you know how I'd react under pressure?"

"I don't. Not for sure. But who does? I've seen guys, born killers with years of experience, get into a situation which looks the same as a hundred others, and lose their shit before you can blink. Nobody's a sure thing."

"But some are surer than others," I murmured.

He ceded the point with a nod, then sighed. "I don't want my guys involved. This has to stay secret. If I put one of my men on the job, there's a much greater chance that they'll be spotted, that word will spread, that they'll be pegged. The people of my world are alert to the movements of their own kind. But you're not one of us. Nobody's watching out for you."

"I'm an invisible man," I said.

He beamed. "Exactly. If you turn me down, and I have to use Rabbit or someone like him, it won't be the end of the world, but you're my first choice because you're someone nobody will expect."

I still didn't like it, but I was beginning to understand it.

"This girl. Toni. What would I have to do with her?"

"Stay with her. Guard her."

"Can I keep her inside my flat the whole time?"

He snorted. "If you can persuade her to stay in, it would be the ideal scenario, but I doubt she'll go for that. She's young and into the whole *joie de vivre* shit. She'll want to hit the town, and I don't have the authority to order her to do otherwise. You'll have to deal with it if she insists on going out, show her the sights and be her chaperone, but try to stick to places *you* know. Don't go anywhere she'll be recognised. Maybe take her to Fervent Eld's gym. The dogs. Your local boozer."

"And if she tries to ditch me?"

"She won't. She agreed to let me provide her with an escort. She might give you grief – she's a fiery, prickly little thing – but she trusts me, so she'll trust you. If she proves me wrong, gives you the shake and goes off by herself, it'll be her fault and I won't hold you accountable for anything that happens to her. We can't save those who work overtime to screw themselves."

"What if something goes wrong, if we get made and have to flee? How do I contact you?"

"I'll give you my number. You can call any time. If the shit hits the fan, I'll make new arrangements, take her off your hands."

"I'd still get paid?" I asked sceptically.

"You get paid in advance," he said. "The full amount. I won't look for it back, no matter what happens."

I did a double take. In advance? I imagined the money sitting in my account, waking up Monday morning in a completely different position to where I was right now and had been for the last few months.

Snap decision, and if it was the dumbest move I'd ever made, so be it.

"I'd want a gun," I told him. "Hi-Power. You get it back when I'm finished."

"That won't be a problem."

"And no double-crosses."

"Hey, I'm a man of –" he started to say, playing the innocent.

"I mean it." I put the bottle down on the desk. "I won't be played. If you try to cross me, I'll come after you. And I'll find you. And I'll make you pay."

"No." He shook his head. "If I was planning something like that, you wouldn't survive the cross. You don't have the resources that I have. If I wanted to betray you, there's nothing you could do to hurt me, and don't kid yourself otherwise. But I don't want to stick a knife in your back. Why should I, after what you did for me? This is about repaying a debt, not punishing a stooge. If you don't believe me, walk away now."

But of course, with a neat little speech like that, and twenty-five thousand notes to back it up, I wasn't about to turn him down.

"Tell me more about the sort of stuff she's into," I said.

And I sat back, and listened, and thought about the money. And I dreamed.

FOUR — THE MOLL

Rabbit drove me back. Didn't say much along the way. I was starting to warm to him. I liked a guy who could keep his own counsel.

Brue had offered cash, but I didn't fancy sitting on that much, worried it would be stolen. At the same time I didn't want to give a sizeable chunk of it to the taxman. The gangster understood my dilemma and had an easy solution for it. He logged in to an online bank account, some private bank I'd never heard of, then passed his phone to me and instructed me to reset the username and password, and also enter my own name, phone number and email address.

"That account's yours now," he said, grinning as he watched me slowly tap in numbers with my right index finger, "or will be if you ever finish typing."

"I was a boxer, not a secretary," I growled.

"Only you have access to it from now on," he said once I'd logged out, logged in again to check I'd done it right, then logged out again. "I can never recover it, short of breaking your legs to make you tell me the details."

"I wish it was that easy to deal with my local bank," I muttered.

"Money tends to speed these things along," Brue smirked. "I'll transfer the funds and email you the bank link while you're on your way home, so that you can download the app to your own devices. You can make payments from it like from any normal account, or pay in if you ever want to top it up. Also, you'll find a link in the main menu, listing all the bank branches around the world where you can walk in and make a cash withdrawal — there aren't that many of them, but you're never too far from one in any of the major cities. All you'll need is the account info and photo ID. They won't ask for anything else, you can withdraw as much as you like, and nothing will be recorded. Revenue and Customs will never know about this."

"You're sure about that?" I asked uneasily.

"You can take it to the bank," he said, and laughed the delighted laugh of a man who thinks he's perfectly placed to put Oscar Wilde out of business.

It took me a long time to fall asleep when Rabbit dropped me off and I climbed the stairs to bed. Thinking about the deal I'd struck, how crazy this was, wanting to call Lewis Brue and cancel.

Remembering my chat with the gang, my admission to myself that I'd maybe picked up Brue in the hope of getting caught in the crossfire. Looking at the place on the wall where I'd hung the two photos all those years ago. Only up there a few weeks while I gingerly pieced myself back together and established my fragile plans for the future, but I could still imagine them hanging there if I squinted.

This could screw me. If I got in over my head, my journey could very feasibly end here, this weekend.

Was that what I secretly wanted? This had been a largely joyless world for me since the desert. Dave and the gang numbed me to some of the pain. So did Fervent and his boys in the gym. But mostly I was out there on the streets in the cab, or staring at the wall in here, lost in the past and suffering. Only one sure, easy way to put an end to all that.

Or was this an attempt to find release another way? If I could make the money work for me, maybe I'd find happiness as a promoter with Fervent. Perhaps this could be the new start I needed, escape at last.

I fell asleep still pondering it, and I wasn't any more certain of my motives when I woke just a few hours later. But I didn't reach for my phone to call Lewis Brue. I was going ahead with this, as crazy as it was, whatever my real reason might be. That much I was sure of. That much and no more.

I went down to tell Dixie about the temporary lodger. Dixie was my landlady. She'd owned and lived in the original building, before going into partnership with a firm of developers years ago to convert it into a block of flats. She could have taken the money and retired to the country, but she liked the neighbourhood and watching it change, so she'd stayed on in one of the new flats (a much larger and nicer flat than mine, it must be said) as landlady in residence.

Dixie Twist was a cool old lady, into the blues and silent movies. Spent her free time composing scores for ancient films that nobody cared about. I'd gone to a few showings in tiny cinemas and dusty old theatres. The blues had never done much for me but I'd always been interested in movies. The silents were a mixed bag, but I saw at least one – *Sunrise* – which was an out-and-out classic. I was hoping to see more over the coming years, but Dixie didn't get out with them too often, partly because they took so long to score, partly because it was difficult finding somewhere to host the events.

"How long will she be staying?" Dixie asked when I told her

about my guest.

"Just until Sunday."

"OK, but no condoms in the toilet. They jam the works and then I have to call the plumber and that's embarrassing for everybody."

"Hey, I told you, she's my cousin."

"Yeah? How old is she?"

"Early twenties," I said, repeating what Brue had told me.

"Hmm. Amazing how many pretty female *cousins* there are around that age."

I scowled. "Would I be telling you about her if she wasn't on the level?"

Dixie laughed. "It's fine, Eyrie. I'm just pulling your leg. You didn't need to tell me, but I'm pleased that you did."

Dixie was right — I hadn't needed to let her know about the girl. But she paid attention to who came and went. I was worried she might spot Toni when I wasn't with her, think she was an intruder, maybe call the police. Unlikely, but I didn't plan to take any chances.

I kept a clean, orderly apartment – a throwback to my Army days – so I didn't have to do much to get it ready. I cleared out the laundry bin, gave the kitchen a rub with a sponge, ran Henry the Hoover around for a while.

I spent the rest of the day nervously killing time. Fixed the front door myself, putting the receipt for the new lock in my wallet to give to Lewis Brue on Sunday when I returned the girl. Watched a movie, *The Devil Thumbs a Ride*, a little-known gem from the 1940s. Rang Dave to let him know I wouldn't be working for the next few nights. I could tell he thought I was going on a bender and I didn't try to convince him otherwise. If this worked out, I'd let him and the others go on thinking of this as one of my lost weekends. I didn't plan to share the true story with them, wary of Lewis Brue's warning to keep it to myself.

Eventually, having wanted to do it all day, I accessed the email that Brue had sent, downloaded the app to my phone and logged in to the account, half-hoping there'd be nothing there, so I'd have a legitimate excuse to call Brue and cancel.

The money had hit as promised. Twenty-five thousand pounds, mine to do with whatever I pleased.

I felt sick as I stared at the numbers. Depressed, almost.

I logged out. Thought yet again about ringing Brue to call this off.

Instead I logged back in and studied the numbers some more.

And this time I started to smile.

She rang three times, long, steady presses on the bell. Strolled straight in when I opened the door, pulling a small wheelie case. She looked shapeless, lost in the folds of a crumpled mac which was several sizes too large for her. A cap pulled down over her ears. Drab trainers. Lightly shaded glasses.

She walked past and scoped the flat before saying anything. Grunted sourly to indicate this wasn't what she was accustomed to. Took off the cap. She had brown hair, shaved in tight and ugly, either by an amateur or a stylist who had been trying to make some sort of a statement. A thin face, narrow cheeks, hardly any spare flesh. She wasn't wearing much make up. Alert green eyes.

She extracted a gun from inside the mac and passed it to me without a word. The Hi-Power that I'd asked for. Next she handed me a flower-patterned bag filled with spare clips, that she'd also been carrying within the coat. As I was stowing the gun and ammo, she produced a tube of lipstick and painted her lips. Checked them on the blank TV screen, then took off her coat. Her dress wasn't going to win any fashion awards, but nobody looking at her would be that bothered about the dress. She was a touch short, nothing a pair of heels couldn't correct. Lithe like an athlete, lightly tanned. Drape her in designer gear, wrap a scarf around the head, give a beautician half an hour with her, and you'd have a beautiful young woman on your hands.

"You the guy?" she asked. She had a northern accent but I couldn't place it.

"I'm *a* guy," I answered.

"Don't get smart," she snapped. "Are you the guy Lewis has provided for me?"

"I hope so." I nodded at the bag with the gun. "You're in trouble if I'm not."

She rolled her eyes. "And this is the pit where I have to waste the next three days of my life?"

"If you don't like it, take a hike," I said sweetly.

That surprised her. She subjected me to a quick once-over, not having expected such an acidic response from the hired help. "You know who I am?" she asked.

"I haven't a clue."

"Lewis didn't tell you?"

"No."

"But you work for him, so you must have some idea."

"No and no."

She frowned. "You don't work for him?"

"I'm just an acquaintance."

"And you've really no idea who I am?"

"I'm not being paid to have ideas."

She laughed and sat on the couch. Dropped her case and kicked it clear of her feet. Raised a hand to control her hair. Stopped when she remembered it had been shorn short. That told me it had been cut very recently. Maybe to help her keep a low profile. But I didn't think too much about that, or who she might be hiding from. Like I'd said, I wasn't being paid to think.

"So what's the deal?" she asked, lifting her legs and stretching out in that catlike way that certain graceful women have, getting the feel of the couch, even though it was far from befitting of her beauty.

"The deal is, Lewis paid me to watch over you," I said, trying not to stare. There had been some women since Zahra, but not many, and none on Toni's level. "He owes me a favour and this is his way of paying me back."

She glanced up sharply. "*Paying you back?* What the hell does that mean? You think he's giving me to you, that I'm your sex toy?"

"No," I blinked, stung by the hostility.

"That's what it sounded like to me," she snapped.

"I'm sorry if it came out that way," I said sincerely. "All I meant was that he's paying me very handsomely to look after you, and I'm grateful to him for his generosity, but I'm under no obligation to do this."

"So I've got to be nice to you?" she bristled.

"Just respectful. Hell, not even that. Just don't make any cutting remarks about my home. It's not much, but it's mine."

"And if I say screw that and tell you it's a dump, you'll throw me out?"

"Yes," I said evenly. "I'd rather not give back the money, but it will be an easy thing to return if I decide the job's more hassle than it's worth."

"Kind of a sensitive fellow, aren't you?" she pouted.

"Just letting you know where we stand. So we don't get off on the wrong foot."

She nodded. "OK. I can see you're thin-skinned, so I'll say no more about your lovely palace of a home. What's the schedule?"

"We stay here and get to know one another."

"Sounds exciting," she yawned. "You want to start?"

"Happy to. I'm Eyrie Brown."

"Eerie? As in...?" She made a ghostly keening sound.

"No. As in what eagles nest in."

"You're making that up," she said.

"My mother had a brother who liked birds," I muttered, and for the first time in years I blushed while defending my ludicrous name.

"Must have fucking loved them," she laughed.

I shrugged, feeling like I was thirteen years old again and taking a slagging in the school yard. "We get what we're given. What about you?"

"Toni Curtis," she said.

"Now you're the one making up names," I smiled.

"Something wrong with my name?" She stared at me coldly.

"No. It's fabulous. But..."

"The actor," she sneered. "Yeah, you're not the first to point it out."

"Is it your real name, or are you just a big Tony Curtis fan?" I asked.

"That's for me to know and you to find out," she sniffed. She tossed her head, meaning to shake her hair haughtily, again forgetting that she didn't have any flowing locks. Scowling, she said, "And if you think I'm staying in all the time, you're deluded. I'm tired tonight, so I don't mind a quiet one, but Fridays and Saturdays are for partying. Tomorrow, I want out, and I know Lewis told you that wasn't a problem, so don't act like it is."

"OK," I sighed. "What do you like doing?"

"Screwing," she replied promptly, to get a reaction. I disappointed her. I'd given lifts to hundreds of girls her age and younger, always testing and teasing, so I was experienced enough to handle such a jab without blinking.

"Then I guess it's gonna be a pretty boring weekend, as that's not on the agenda," I said. "Anything else? Opera, ballet, a nice church service?"

"Fucking comedian," she mumbled. "Have you got anything to drink?"

"Like what?"

"Champagne?"

"Only if they've started piping it through the taps."

"Wine?"

"Sorry."

"Christ. What about beer? If Brue's put me in with a teetotaller, I'll choke the bastard to death."

"I've got beer," I comforted her.

"Hallelujah. Spirits?"

"Rum."

"Eyrie Brown, I love you."

"I'll get a bottle," I said, bemused.

She stood. "Just point the way. I like to mix my drinks myself. Men are no good at mixing drinks. They're –"

"Let me guess," I interrupted, reading her mind by the way her lips were lifting at the edges. "They're only good for one thing, right?"

She winked and said, "Sometimes not even that."

Then she headed for the fridge, leaving me to shake my head and prepare for what looked set to be a lively three days.

She drank too much, too fast. A double rum with a beer chaser, gone in a few greedy gulps. Repeat. Licking her lips and commending me on the quality of my rum as she poured again. I found it amusing and waited for the kicker. If she thought I was going to clean up her vomit...

Turned out she was the sort who didn't get sick. She was the sort who got angry. Sat there telling me how shitty the world was, how lousy people were, she didn't give a fuck, she was going to make something of herself, she was better than the rest of those bastards, she was going places.

"You know what I *really* enjoy?" she asked, eyes twinkling mischievously. The dress was now hitched up around her knees, which were swaying gently. Nothing too overt, but certainly deliberate. I ignored the bare flesh as best I could.

"I doubt I'll need three guesses," I said drily.

"Not *that*," she giggled. "Though that's fun too." She ran a calculating eye over me, looking for a reaction. Shrugged when she didn't get one. "Fights," she said.

"Boxing?" I was interested for the first time.

She laughed. "Fuck, no. I mean real fights. Dogs, cockerels, badgers. You ever see badgers fight?"

"No," I said with disdain.

"Me neither, but I've heard it's awesome. I was supposed to go to a badger fight last week but it got busted by some journalist."

"What a pity."

She cocked her head, noting my disapproval. "You don't like it?"

"No."

"You don't look like an animal rights activist."

"I'm not. I just don't like exploitation. Animals in that situation don't have any say in the matter. It's like whoring out a child."

"You reckon?" she hummed, pouring another drink. "But an animal's not a person. They're born to fight. That's what they'd be doing in the wild. Besides, they'll only end up in a burger or hot dog."

"They don't put badgers in burgers," I told her.

"How little you know," she giggled. Then she looked at me seriously. "I admire your analogy. *Whoring out a child*. That's exactly what it's like. Sick fucks."

I stared at her, confused. "I don't understand. You said…"

"I was messing with you," she said without any remorse. Clicked her tongue. "No, more than that, I was testing you. Some guys will play along with anything if they think it's gonna get them in a girl's knickers."

"I'm not trying to –" I started to retort angrily.

"I know, I know," she soothed me, "but I wanted to be sure. I figured I'd run it by you, see how it played. I'm glad you're not one of those creeps who gets off on animal cruelty. I've no time for those bastards. I was with a guy a while back – must be why I thought of that particular ruse – who *was* into it. I'd been paid to get close to him. There was a deal going down and..."

She waved a hand dismissively.

"That doesn't matter," she continued. "But when it came time to kiss his cheek and say goodbye, I drugged him and tied him up. Left him in an abandoned barn, naked from the waist down, with a couple of fighting dogs. I fed them before I jumped ship, so they were nice and placid when I waved *adieu*, but they get hungry real quickly, so when it came time for their next meal..."

She chuckled viciously. I had no idea if it was a true story or if she was trying to test me again, so I kept a stony face and said nothing. But I was glad she wasn't into the animal stuff. I'd have had a hard time justifying this job to myself if she had been.

"I do actually love boxing," she said after a pause. "Two guys in a ring, who've chosen to be there, beating each other to a pulp..." She lay back and let the glass rest on her thighs. Rolled it meaningfully between her hands. "It gets me hot. The blood, the battle, the fevered look in their eyes, everyone in the crowd excited, betting, yelling. I sometimes want to do it right there and then, strip off and start fucking in the seats while the guys are hammering it out on the canvas. I reckon no one would notice. They'd be too busy watching the fight."

"I wouldn't put that theory to the test if I was you," I sniffed.

"Prude," she laughed.

"Does Brue take you to the fights?" I asked.

"No, he..." She stopped. "He told me not to talk about him. Told me the less you knew, the better. Said you wouldn't ask too many questions anyway, and to be suspicious if you did."

"Fair enough."

"Should I be suspicious, Eyrie Brown?" she asked mockingly.

I didn't reply. It was nearly two in the morning. My eyes were starting to droop. I should have nabbed a couple more hours sleep earlier.

She rose from the couch and walked round the room, checking it out again, glass in hand. She moved fluidly, even though she'd had too much to drink. Examined my posters. One of the cast of *Casablanca*, one of Rita Hayworth, a couple of Ali, the Greatest, my hero when I was a child.

She found my DVD collection and bent to examine the discs, not expecting much by the look on her face. After a few seconds she squealed and plucked out my copy of *Some Like It Hot*, one of the first films I'd replaced when my previous collection had gone walkabout.

"I don't believe it! And *Sweet Smell of Success*. And *The Defiant Ones*. You're a Tony Curtis fan?"

"Not really," I said. "Just three great films he happened to be in. He was a good actor but he turned up in crap most of the time."

"Bite your tongue!" she shouted. "Every one of his films is a classic. God, he was handsome. Why can't they build them like him any more? I was born decades too late."

It looked like my earlier question, about whether Toni Curtis was her real name or if she'd chosen it because she liked the actor, had been answered.

Toni took the disc to the DVD player, switched on the TV – "How old *is* this gargantuan piece of shit? Did they lower it in place with a crane, then build the flat around it? Has no one told you we're living in the twenty-first century?" – and fast-forwarded to the first appearance of Curtis and Jack Lemmon. Sat on the floor, gazing at her idol, beaming happily while I stared at her, surprised that she'd casually drop a word like gargantuan into the conversation, telling myself to be careful not to jump to any conclusions about this loud and bloodthirsty but far from stupid young woman with an apparent good taste in movies.

"Look at him," she crowed. "He was so young then, so beautiful. Hell, even in a dress he looked amazing. If a woman turned up looking like that, I'd go lesbian for her, the hell with men."

I moved over so that I could see the screen. I'd always thought Lemmon was the better of the pair. Certainly made a lot more quality movies than Curtis. But there are times to voice an opinion and there are times to keep it to yourself.

"This is my favourite film of all time," she told me. "I saw it when I was twelve. That's when I changed my name. I fell in love with him and thought if I took his name, maybe I'd end up looking that good too. I wised up when I got older but I never fell out of love or swapped my name back. Changed it legally when I was old enough, only I use an *i* instead of a *y*. More feminine, you know?"

"The end's my favourite bit," I told her. "When they're speeding away in the boat and the old guy says –"

"*Nobody's perfect!*" She laughed. "That's a top line, but it would have been better coming from Tony, if he'd shouted it over his shoulder. The old guy was a nobody. Why should he get a zinger of a line like that?"

"Tony was too busy with Marilyn Monroe to be saying anything."

"Marilyn," she snorted. "I never saw the big deal. You know what gets my goat? When you see posters and adverts for *Some Like It Hot* and she's centre stage, top billing, Tony and Lemmon in the background, like a couple of extras. She was the spare in that movie. They were the stars. Tony made it, not Marilyn."

"Lots of people wouldn't agree with you," I said, watching as the camera followed Marilyn's hemline at a viewer-friendly angle. "I'd be one of them," I admitted, drooling ever so slightly.

Toni caught my expression and grinned. A sexy, serious grin. "You know," she said, her voice rising innocently, "I think *I'm* better looking than Marilyn. Not so much the hips or legs, but I've better tits, don't you reckon?" She jutted her chest out and smiled as though she didn't know what she was doing.

I said nothing.

"Of course, you can't really see with this bra," she mused. "It makes them look smaller than they are. Hold on a sec and I'll take it off." Her hands snaked up around her back.

"Wait," I said softly.

I slid in front of her, blocking the screen. She let her head fall back and gazed up. I smiled. Leant over.

And slapped her face.

It was a gentle slap. The way you'd casually slap a child's bum in the old days, when it wasn't a crime. I wouldn't normally hit a woman, even a light slap like that, but I had to let her know there were boundaries. She was playing with me, but games of that kind have a nasty habit of spiralling out of control, and I wasn't going to put myself in a position where I'd end up screwing a girl who was involved with the likes of Lewis Brue. I wasn't suicidal.

Toni changed instantly. Pushed me away. Shot to her feet, smile vanishing. Her right hand shot into a pocket that I hadn't taken any notice of, came out with a blade. She lashed at me. Would have drawn blood if I hadn't been quick enough stepping back.

"You bastard!" she shouted. "Nobody hits –"

I pulled the Hi-Power. I'd removed it from the bag earlier, loaded it and kept it on me since, figuring I should have it on my person as long as I was standing guard over her, just to be safe.

She stopped talking when she saw the gun. Stopped advancing. Stared.

"I'll be careful if I have to shoot," I told her. "I won't hit the bone, just a flesh wound, but it will be enough to halt you in your tracks. Then I'll tie you up, ring Brue to see what he wants done with you – if he wants me to keep you like that, or send someone to fetch you and take charge of you for the rest of the weekend – and that will be that. Your choice. Drop the knife. I don't give second warnings. I'll take hesitation as a sign of non-compliance."

She dropped it and slumped to the floor, eyes only for me now, Tony and the rest of the *Some Like It Hot* gang temporarily forgotten.

"You're dead," she said softly.

"No," I told her. "If I'd let you take that bra off, if I'd gone along with your game, if I'd let my prick lead my brain, *then* I'd be dead. I'm no expert, but I'm pretty sure rule number one in a situation like this is, 'Don't screw the employer's woman.' I've been paid to protect you and that's all I'm going to do."

"I'll tell Lewis you beat me and raped me."

I shrugged. "Maybe he'll believe you. And maybe the last thing I'll see before I die will be my own manhood dangling before my eyes. But I don't think so. I don't know much about Lewis Brue, but I doubt he would have picked me if he thought there was any chance I'd jump your bones. You can tell him your story if you like. Then I'll tell him mine and take my chances."

She hung her head. For a moment I thought she was going to cry.

Instead she laughed.

"OK," she said, picking up the remote, which was the size of a small Bible. "We know where we stand. You're in charge and you've laid the ground rules. Fine. I'll stick by them. No more flirting. I'll do what you say and you won't hit me again."

"Sounds reasonable."

"Because if you do..." she warned. "If you ever strike me, or trip me, or look at me the wrong way..." She pulled a tiny gun, faster than I was expecting, from another pocket, and levelled it at my face. Kept it on me for what felt like a long time before lowering it and returning it to its resting place.

"...I'll kill you," she said simply.

And I had no doubt that she meant it.

And I was suddenly very glad I hadn't slapped her any harder.

Toni was quieter the rest of the night. She was still pissed at me for slapping her, but I think she felt bad for having played the seductive vixen. She knew what Lewis Brue would do to me if I made a move on her. She felt guilty for having toyed with me and tempting me, knowing what the end result would have been if I'd given in to temptation.

At least that's what I liked to think.

The other possibility was that she was simply bored.

She sat watching *Some Like It Hot* and drinking. Replayed the film from its start when it finished. Pulled her knife and started picking her nails with it, telling me all the things she'd do to Marilyn if she could travel back in time and get her hands on her. She really had it in for the actress. Outraged when Marilyn kissed Tony Curtis. She threw the knife at the screen. It bounced off harmlessly because by that stage she was too drunk to put any strength into the throw.

I said as little as possible, waiting for her to pass out, which she did shortly after four in the morning. When I heard the soft snores, I picked her up and carried her to the bedroom. Laid her on the bed and pulled the duvet over her. I was tempted to undress her, to give her a shock when she woke, but figured she might not take the joke well and, if she woke before me, maybe she'd decide to pay me back by slitting my throat — from what I'd seen, I wouldn't have put that past her.

I rolled the suitcase into the bedroom and left it there. Poured a large glass of water for her, then another, and left them on the bedside table. Then I took the couch in the living room and settled back for the night. The couch didn't pull out into a bed, and it was an uncomfortable piece of crap – nobody ever stayed over, so I'd never really needed to upgrade – but, for twenty-five thousand pounds, I'd have happily slept on the toilet.

FIVE — RINGSIDE

I woke around midday, showered, shaved, cleared away the empties from the night before, then relaxed and tried to read some old magazines which I keep in stock for quiet moments like these, but I couldn't concentrate.

Thoughts turned to Zahra, and I found myself comparing her with Toni. Two very different women. Zahra was far more conservative and modest than the young lady sleeping in my bed. Nowhere near as visually striking as Toni, though she'd been beautiful to me.

I tried to imagine Zahra sharing this flat with me, but I could never picture her living here. If we'd had our whole lives to share, I'd have settled in the desert. I wouldn't have brought her to London. This city would have changed her, and I didn't want her to change. To me, she'd been perfect as she was.

It was after two when Toni showed her face. She looked a state when she staggered in from the bedroom. Her face was a mess and she'd kicked off the dress sometime in the night, replacing it with a baggy top. The top covered her knickers but only just. She moved slowly, scowling grumpily, hungover.

"What time is it?" she croaked.

"Time you were getting dressed," I said.

She glanced at her bare legs and managed a wan grin. "Don't hit me, boss," she giggled. Then she fell into a chair and groaned. "I feel like shit."

"I wonder why?"

"Shut up. It's not the drink. It's a bug or something."

"Right. The rum and beer bug. A lot of that about. Eat some

bread and drink lots of water. You'll be fine in a couple of hours."

"I don't want to even think about moving." She opened her eyes and smiled sweetly at me. "Would you be a dear?"

"No," I smiled back just as sweetly. "I'm a bodyguard, not a servant. You want something, get it yourself."

"You're a real gentleman, Eyrie Brown," she sneered. "Full of the milk of human kindness. I bet you do lots of charity work in your spare time."

"I sure do. And every penny raised goes to the FEBB benefit fund."

"The what?"

"FEBB," I repeated.

"Which stands for?"

"Fuck Everybody But Brown."

She laughed. "That's pretty good."

"It should be," I told her. "I stole it from W.C. Fields."

"Who?"

I rolled my eyes at the ceiling. The youth of today! Then again, I wouldn't have known about Fields either if it wasn't for Dixie, who'd introduced me to some of his silent shorts, before I went on to relish him in his talkies heyday. His voice alone was enough to make me smile.

"Go on," I said. "Fill your stomach. I'd advise a couple of raw eggs if you feel up to it."

"Advise all you want," she said, getting up and scratching one of her lean, pale thighs. "I don't eat boiled eggs, never mind raw. Jesus. Eating something that's come out of a chicken's..." She blanched and wandered off to the kitchen. I switched on the

TV, trying to distract myself, so that I wouldn't dwell on the image of that short top riding up those long legs.

Women. They should come with warning labels.

The afternoon was dragging. Toni had come through the worst of her hangover but was bored. I suggested we watch a film but she'd had enough of "that old tank of a TV set," saying she needed something *hi-def*, that all those fat, flickering pixels had messed with her eyes, and that was why her head hurt so bad.

I bypassed the opportunity to have another dig at her refusal to accept that she had only her excessive alcohol consumption to blame for her sorry condition.

Instead I started thinking of what I could do with her. I didn't want to take her out on the town yet — it was too early for pubs and clubs. The gym was an option, but I could predict the distraction she'd create, and Fervent wouldn't thank me for that. Shopping? I had no idea what stores would be deemed appropriate, and didn't fancy jostling for elbow room with the Friday crowds.

Then, inspired by my earlier mention of W.C. Fields, I had a thought. "Put some trousers on," I told Toni. "We're going downstairs."

"Why?" she frowned.

"To mug a little old lady," I deadpanned.

Toni grumbled but found some baggy trousers to match the top. She pulled on a pair of trainers – no socks – and followed me down the stairs, looking several years younger than she had last night, like a surly teenager who was being forced to go on a museum trip.

Dixie was surprised to see me when she opened the door. "I thought you were otherwise engaged this weekend," she said.

"I wanted to introduce you to my cousin," I said, stepping aside to reveal a confused Toni hovering close behind me.

Dixie studied the blinking girl and sniffed. "Still sticking with the cousin line?"

"Like glue," I smiled.

"Then come on in, *cousin*," she said to Toni, and ushered us inside.

I'm not sure how I expected the visit to go. I think I took Toni down there to punish her, figuring she'd have to sit quietly and suffer the visit in agonised silence, smiling fakely while her head thumped inside. But to my surprise she took to Dixie swiftly and genuinely.

It started with a poster for *Metropolis*, one of the better-known silent films that Dixie had scored. She'd played with it several times, not only in London but at film festivals abroad. The poster featured the iconic image of a female robot set against towering skyscrapers. I'd hazard a guess that, along with Chaplin's *Little Tramp*, *Metropolis* is probably the most widely recognised remnant of silent cinema, not least because of the boost it got back in the 1980s when Queen used clips from it in their *Radio Ga Ga* video.

Of course the 1980s were a far-flung historical era for Toni, and I doubted she was even familiar with Queen the band, never mind their video catalogue. So when she spotted the framed poster and said, "That's pretty cool," I got ready to explain. Luckily Toni moved on to her next sentence before I could speak up and spared me the embarrassment of looking like a condescending idiot.

"I'm guessing it's not an original 4 sheet," she said.

Dixie sighed. "If only. But no, it's a modern reproduction."

"Have you seen the movie," Toni asked, "or do you just like the poster?"

"Seen it many times, and scored it," Dixie replied.

"Scored it?"

"I score old silent movies and play along with them at screenings."

"No way!" Toni exclaimed. "That must be the coolest job in the world."

"Unfortunately it's not a job as such," Dixie chuckled, "but yes, I can't think of anything cooler."

And they were off.

Toni didn't know anywhere near as much about silent films as she did about the movies of Tony Curtis, but she'd seen a few Chaplin features, had watched lots of Harold Lloyd shorts, and was a fan of *Metropolis*, even though she admitted that she'd only ever viewed it in chunks, finding it too hard to sit through the entire film in one go.

"Silent films can be hard for a modern audience to engage with," Dixie said. "They were an art form, and if you don't watch lots of them, it's tricky to connect. It's easier when you see one in a cinema, where you're forced to properly focus."

"You're not doing one tonight, are you?" Toni asked, excited.

"I'm afraid not," Dixie said, "but I can let Eyrie know the next time I have a show lined up, and pass him on a couple of tickets."

That would have been perfect, if we could have spent the night in a dark old cinema, but the fates are seldom that kind.

We spent the next couple of hours with Dixie. The ladies chatted about old movies, music, fashion, politics and the housing market. To my astonishment, Toni was far more informed than I'd assumed, and it served as a timely reminder of one of Fervent Eld's favourite clichés — *To assume makes an ass of u and me.* (Or, as a real cousin of mine had once rib-ticklingly misquoted, *To* presume *makes an ass of u and me.*)

Toni didn't put on any kind of a sweet, innocent act – she cursed freely, was harsh on those politicians she disagreed with, told a few lewd jokes that made me blush even while Dixie was laughing with delight – but she was honest and open and warm and... nice.

It wasn't what I'd expected from my young ward, and I found myself glancing at her every so often when she was talking animatedly, once again comparing her with Zahra, as I had earlier in the day, but much more favourably this time.

In those moments I forced myself to recall who she was and what she might be. She was part of Lewis Brue's world, and while I had no idea what role she occupied in it, I was pretty sure she wasn't a companion for sweet old ladies.

It would be easy to fall for the woman I was seeing here in Dixie's flat.

I warned myself not to, and hoped I'd be wise enough to heed that warning.

It was all hugs and air kisses when we bade goodbye to Dixie, who grabbed me by the arm as I was leaving and whispered, "Cousin or not, I approve. Bring her by again any time."

It hadn't been the afternoon I'd expected, but I'd enjoyed it, and Toni had too. She was much brighter than when we'd trudged down the stairs, and there was no more teasing, no flashes of thigh, no bitchy comments about my TV.

She disappeared to prepare for the night ahead, and when she re-emerged around seven, she was a different person. Had her face on. A short blue dress and tight top which left her midriff bare. Sheer tights with a spider's web pattern worked into them. A necklace, rings and bangles which maybe cost more than I was being paid to take care of her. High heels to make the most of her long legs. The night before, I'd assumed she'd look drop-dead gorgeous when she made the effort. Now I knew for sure.

The only thing detracting from the overall effect was the hair. She'd brushed it as artfully as she could, but there wasn't much there to style. I could tell she was angry about her shaven locks, and wondered what the story was — I had a feeling she hadn't volunteered for the haircut.

"How do I look?" she asked, twirling for me.

"Hot as lava," I admitted. "Everything a man could ever want and more." She beamed, delighted with the compliment. "Now take it all off."

"What?" Her smile crumpled.

"The jewellery, the shoes, the tights, the top — put them back in the suitcase. You can keep the dress but the rest has to go."

"Why?" she snarled, readying herself for a fight.

"Because you're with Eyrie Brown tonight, not Lewis Brue," I explained. "I'm a cabbie. I make good money, but only by the average Joe's standards. The women I've been with could never have afforded to deck themselves up like this. My kind of people and your kind of people only hook up in the movies. If I go out with a pretty young thing on my arm, it's not beyond the realm of possibility. Some of the guys I know have girlfriends and wives who could pass for models. People will say I've landed on my feet and think no more about it. But if I strut around with a woman dressed like a Trump wife, they'll look closer and ask questions."

"And we don't want any questions." She nodded grudgingly. "You make a good argument."

She headed back into the bedroom, already taking off the earrings and necklace. Returned in a blouse, plain tights and a more sensible pair of shoes. She'd also wrapped a bandana round her head, to make her look more street.

"Better?" she asked.

"Perfect."

I gazed at her curiously.

"What?" she huffed.

"How did you pack so much stuff into one small suitcase?"

"We ladies have our ways," she smirked, then clapped and stretched. "So, you ready to hit the bright lights?"

"In a while."

"How long?"

"Another hour or so."

"Why the wait? I'm ready to go."

"I'm taking you somewhere special. It won't be open yet."

"A surprise." Her eyes glittered. "I like surprises."

She settled down in the front of the TV and surfed the Freeview channels, muttering darkly about my being a cheapskate and not knowing anyone else in the world who didn't have Netflix. We seemed to be coming out of the Dixie Twist honeymoon period and back to normal.

"Just watch it on your phone if you miss it that much," I snapped.

"Do you see any phone?" she snapped back. "Lewis made me leave it behind. He didn't trust me not to blow my location. So I'm stuck with that freak of a thing from the Ice Age." She pointed at my sad behemoth of a TV set.

I chuckled, ducked into the bathroom and rang Fervent Eld to make sure the venue hadn't changed. My guest might be feeling like a terrible injustice had been perpetrated, but I didn't think she'd be mourning the loss of her phone a few hours from now.

"Where are we going?" she asked as I navigated the streets of London's East End.

"You'll see when we get there."

I'd borrowed a car from Larry, a dealer I'd been friends with since school. He sold second-hand wrecks, though he'd sworn this one was kosher, cherry-picked from among the duds, because we were mates. It was rumoured the cars were a front for dealing of an entirely different kind. I didn't pay any attention to those tales, though it wouldn't have surprised me if they were true — Larry had always been a wide boy, the guy you went to in school if were going clubbing and wanted a few pills to add to the party atmosphere.

It was early, but already the East End had come alive with the creatures of the night. Street hookers hogging the corners. Dealers peddling their wares while the cops drove by and looked the other way. Kids learning to smoke, to push, to steal. Every pick-pocket busy. Gangs parading their colours. Tourists hurrying back to their hotels, understanding too late why they'd been offered such wonderful deals on their rooms.

Or maybe that was just the side of London that *I* saw. A city is what you make of it. I'd grown up on these streets, in neighbourhoods where film crews came to produce dark, gritty dramas. And in the Army I'd served in places where you had to scan for danger every time you ventured forth. The East End was probably nowhere near as caustic and seedy as it seemed to me. I was simply seeing it with tired, damaged eyes.

Toni's eyes were anything but tired and damaged, but I had no doubt that she saw the city the same way I did. She clocked everything, every last deal, every picked pocket, every high-class prostitute stepping out of a cab and heading into a four-star hotel.

The difference was, she got a buzz from the action. On one street we saw a couple of hawk-like Eastern Europeans laying into a guy who ate far too much fast food — running away would never be an option for him. They were beating him bad. People walked by as though nothing was happening. You didn't get involved in a scene like that, not unless you were stupid. I turned a blind eye to it, the way everybody else did, but the fight excited her. I saw her cheeks flush and she turned for a lingering view. It was hard to believe that this was the same young woman who had interacted with Dixie so sweetly just a few short hours ago.

"Do you think they'll kill him?" she asked.

"No."

"Why not?"

"He owes them money. You don't kill someone who's in debt to you."

She stared at me. "How do you know he owes them?"

"The way they're beating him. You beat people differently,

depending on what you want. They're giving him a going-over that he'll remember, but steering clear of his vitals. Punching to hurt, not to kill."

"You know a lot about it." She sat up straight when we turned out of sight of the violence. "I thought you were just a cabbie, that you weren't into that kind of thing."

"Street fights aren't *that kind of thing*," I told her. "Everyone here has seen plenty of those. You start to note the finer points after a while."

I took a right and carried on. Toni went on staring at me.

"You got a girlfriend?" she asked.

"Not at the moment."

"How long since your last?"

"A few months, I guess, maybe more."

"Did she leave because you beat her?" Toni smirked.

"Still sore about that?"

"Not sore at all," she said, "but I haven't forgotten. I hope you didn't forget either." She tapped her handbag, and I figured she meant she'd brought the gun with her.

"Don't worry," I grunted. "The *very light* slap was just to focus your attention. As a rule of thumb, I don't hit women."

"Glad to hear it." She turned on the radio and began tapping out the tune on the dashboard. "So, you ready to tell me where we're going?"

"Not yet."

"Christ, Eyrie, is this a mystery ride or something?"

"Something," I said.

"It better be worth the suspense."

I looked over at her cheeks, still flushed with excitement

after her brief glimpse of the street fight.

"It will," I promised.

The hall was almost full, mainly with eager-looking men talking in hushed tones. I looked for Fervent Eld. He spotted me and waved. I pushed through to him, dragging Toni with me. He was near the ring, prepping one of his boys.

Toni saw the ropes and groaned. "A boxing match? You give me the big build-up, and *this* is the payoff? I love boxing, so I won't complain, but you promised me a big surprise and this is just –"

"Hush. It's not a boxing match."

"But –"

"Shh. Hi, Fervent." I shook his hand and clapped the kid on the back. He was from the gym but I couldn't remember his name, he hadn't been coming long. A skinny guy, lightweight, very small hands. In my opinion he wouldn't make much money, even fighting in venues like this.

"Good crowd," I commented.

"Yeah," Fervent replied, ogling the girl. "It's O'Malley versus Redhead Moore. Clash of the mad Micks. Should be a bloodbath. This charming young lady a friend of yours?" He grinned at Toni in a way which would have frightened a more timid soul. She only laughed and stuck out her hand. He bent and kissed it, dirty old charmer that he believed he was.

"I'm no friend of his," Toni purred. "Just using him to get around town for the weekend. Name's Shelley Lean. And you're…?"

"Fervent Eld."

"Nice to meet you, Mr Eld." She smiled and I could hear his back creaking as he stood to full attention. I turned aside so he wouldn't see my smirk. Last time Eld had pulled, knee-high skirts had still been outlawed in many counties.

I could see he wanted to chat, but I gave him a look and we went shuffling away to find a pair of seats. She'd had sense enough to give a false name – though for all I knew, maybe that *was* her real name – but I didn't want her talking to anyone too long, in case she let something slip. I looked around to see if there were any familiar faces I might have to avoid, but they were all strangers.

"What's the deal?" she asked as the first two contestants – Eld's skinny kid and a guy from a different gym – entered the ring.

"They're going to box," I told her.

"But you said –"

"See their hands?"

"I'm not blind."

"See any gloves?"

Her scowl disappeared. "They're going to fight with their bare knuckles, like in the old days?"

"Yeah," I said sourly, "just like in the good old days."

The bell rang and they advanced to the middle of the ring and began hammering each other. Both men had been trained to go for a quick win. This crowd wasn't interested in lightweights. The blood fiends were here for the big guns.

"What are the rules?" Toni asked, bobbing about on her seat like an anxious songbird, so she didn't miss any of the action.

"Roughly the same as normal boxing, except there's no limit to the number of rounds — it goes on until one drops and can't get up. And you get away with more here. You might be jeered for a low blow or biting, but there are no points to be deducted, and the ref only steps in if you go way too far – for instance if you start kicking – or if you don't back off when your opponent's down."

"Hit him!" she screamed, leaping to her feet as Fervent's kid saw a gap in his opponent's defence and smashed through. "Kill the fucker! Beat his brains out!"

As though obeying her crude order, the kid went for the kill, and the fight was over less than a minute later. A couple of guys in Fervent's team raised the kid on their shoulders to a mixture of cheers and laughs, then their coach led him away. A flash wanker in a suit tossed a fifty at the kid and he stooped to scramble after it. Bare-knuckle fighters weren't, for the most part, overly proud. With the exception of a few maniacs who were in it for brutal bragging rights, it was all about the money. I'd gone on my own knees to chase loose notes a couple of times, and thought nothing of it.

"Like the show?" I asked.

"Hell yes." Her face was flushed and I could almost hear her heart beating fast beneath the fabric of her blouse. "How many fights will there be?"

"Depends how long each lasts. If you get a few marathons early on, they'll cancel some of the rest and move on to the main events. They usually finish about midnight, so the punters can hit the clubs and have plenty of time to chat about the night's sparkling entertainment."

There wasn't too much bitterness in my voice. I could understand the crowd's hunger, and I'd taken their money myself, so it wasn't like I could look down my nose at them. It's a hard world. You do what you must to get by. I didn't blame the ghoulish spectators. They spent good money and the boxers needed that cash. Sure, some of the fighters would end up with nothing. They'd do this for a few years, make pennies, retire bloody and scarred, useless for anything thereafter. But that's the luck of the draw. In life, some fly, some dive. A wise man takes what he gets, rolls with the blows as best he can, and leaves others to their own worries. It doesn't pay to have a social conscience. Not in this sort of a city, in these kind of times.

Toni was in her element. Got off on the fighting in a big way. On her feet half the night, shouting and screaming, throwing empty beer cans into the ring when she felt a fighter wasn't giving his all. Nobody minded because she was young and beautiful and they got to admire her curves every time she leapt up and waved. A couple of women tried copying her, but she was the star attraction and nobody showed any interest in her competitors, so they soon quit and sat down to sulk.

The crowd got its money's worth that night. Broken teeth. Shattered bones. The floor awash with blood and strips of flesh.

One enthusiastic Latvian bit the ear off a Turk and spat it out. I think he was trying to hit Toni, who'd been berating him. To my relief it fell short — I shudder to think what she might have done with it.

Another guy kneed his opponent in the groin, only for the offended party to pull a knife that he'd sneaked in. He sliced it deep across his enemy's chest. The ref and trainers got them out of there before either could kill the other, but I was sure they'd take it outside and finish it away from the gaze of the witnesses.

We left before the mad Micks were done with one another.

The men were lumbering hulks, full of hate and blacksmith's muscles, each intent on destruction, but they went about it leisurely, trading punch for punch, content to take their time and grind out a result. I wanted to stay – this was like a proper fight – but Toni was bored.

"Did you see his nipple go flying?" she asked as we exited, referring to the knife-interrupted fight. "If he'd cut lower down, he'd have split the guy's stomach open and his guts would have poured out. That would have been something to see, huh?"

"Yeah," I said drily. "A shame you don't have your phone. You could have taken some photos."

"How come you know about exciting shit like this?" she asked. "You sat there all night with a disapproving frown. Why do you mix with these people if you're so fucking normal?"

"Never said I was normal," I told her as we entered an alley on the way to the car. You couldn't park too close to these places. It didn't do to draw attention. "I used to fight."

"You were a boxer?"

"Yes."

"Bare-knuckles?"

"In the end, yeah."

She stopped and stared at me. I walked on a few paces but she didn't move. I paused and turned.

"What?" I asked defensively.

"You fought in places like this?"

"Yes. I boxed for Fervent, real boxing. Never amounted to much. Did a bit of this later in life, when I needed to make some cash."

She came closer, right up to me, and examined my face.

"You don't look like one of them," she said. "They were rougher. More cuts, scars, bruises."

"I've been out of it a long time," I shrugged. "You heal. Besides, I was one of the better fighters, only rarely took a bad beating. And I had brains enough to quit while I was ahead."

"How good were you?" she asked quietly.

"I was a handy southpaw, won most of my fights." I chuckled ruefully. "But that was no big thing. A lot of the guys who fight bare-knuckle have never boxed legitimately. They're down on their luck, have no other options, come to it when they're in a dark place, no dreams, no ambitions. Some are big and fast, but they have no learnt skills to bring to the ring. I was pretty experienced, so they were rarely fair contests."

She looked me up and down, then grabbed me and pulled me even closer, until our lips were almost touching. "Listen," she whispered hoarsely. "Last night I was just fooling, teasing you, trying to get a reaction, knowing I could play you any way I liked if you made a move on me. Now it's different."

I could feel the kick of her heart as her chest was rammed up against mine. Not the worst feeling in the world.

"Let's go at it like cats, Eyrie. Here. Now." She pulled my hands up so they were on her hips. "I won't ever breathe a word. It'll be our secret. Nothing to do with Lewis. Look at me. You'll see I'm not lying."

And she wasn't, if I was any judge. There was lust in those pretty young eyes. Her blood was boiling and (crude but true) her juices were pumping. She could be mine if I wanted, no comebacks to worry about. A wild fuck, a calming cuddle, and she'd have forgotten about it by morning, never a word to anyone.

"You barely know me," I murmured.

She shrugged. "It's just sex. Doesn't mean much to me."

The only times I'd ever heard someone say that before had been in my fantasies. It was what part of me had been waiting for all my life. An adolescent dream come true. A perfectly formed, exquisitely sculpted woman with all the low sexual morals of a horny teenage boy.

I prised my hands away and took a step back. Smiled regretfully. "No."

"Eyrie, don't be –"

I put a finger to her lips and shook my head. "It would be a mistake."

"But I won't tell. I'm not trying to trick you. I just want –"

"I know," I said kindly. "But it would hang over me forever. You wouldn't mean to say anything, but your tongue could slip one day, or you could talk in your sleep. I know I'm going to regret this for a long, long time – you're the most beautiful woman to ever offer herself to me – but you're not mine. I don't know if you're Lewis Brue's or some other gangster's, but you're certainly not mine. I won't risk my life for a quick screw, not even with someone as stunning as you."

Her shoulders slumped. "Fucking Lewis," she muttered. "Sets me up with the one fucking guy in London who has a level head on his shoulders. OK, Mr Knight In Shining Armour." She looped her arm round mine and smiled. "At least walk me back to the car. Or is this close contact too much for you?"

"This is fine," I told her. "I might even stretch to…" I gave her bum a pat, "…a little bit of a fumbling grope, if the lady has no objections."

"The lady's just fine," she giggled and we walked back to the car, slowly, truly at ease with one another for the first time since she'd knocked on my door the night before.

SIX — A BRAWL

I took her to MURPHY'S for a few drinks. It was a claustrophobic, nasty joint, populated by mean-spirited drunks who liked to scrap over nothing to entertain themselves. You could expect to see tables flying, boots connecting with heads, and knives flashing any normal Friday night. But we arrived shortly after a savage battle, one which had almost gutted the place. The police had been summoned and nearly all of the regulars had been carted off. We stayed for a couple of very quick drinks, but when it became obvious there would be no further action, we moved on to DEL'S.

DEL'S was run by a one-armed gypsy who served his customers with a sneer and wasn't averse to spitting in the odd pint or two. He hired staff for their surly dispositions and it was in all likelihood the least welcoming bar in the entire city. You didn't get many fights here, but it was usually packed with the pick of London's lowlifes, and when it came to people-watching, they didn't come any scuzzier or more luridly fascinating than the locals at DEL'S. I had a hunch Toni would enjoy the walk-of-life show, even if it wasn't *hi-def*.

A couple of tables near the back were reserved for gamblers, and they were always buzzing, fools from all areas of the world coming to take on the infamous in-house card sharks. I was amazed that people found out about this place – you wouldn't find many reviews if you Googled it – but I guess gamblers have their own grapevine.

A large glass tank full of snakes was perched on one end of the bar. Every few weeks or so, some moron would put a fist or foot through it and the joint would have to be evacuated while the snakes were being recovered. That was the only time you'd ever see Del smile, when the snakes were loose and the customers were screaming and running for their lives. Rumour had it, if the tank went too long without getting busted, Del paid a stooge to do the job for him.

Toni's nose wrinkled when we walked in. Del had some sort of a deal going with the health department, because the bar hadn't been cleaned in about six years, yet had never been shut down. The dust was nearly as thick as my TV set in places, and you could have gone for a swim in old beer spills in some areas.

"This is a shithole," Toni complained as we pushed through the crowd to a beer-stained table. (I *hoped* they were only beer stains.)

"You want to leave?" I asked.

"Are you crazy?" she whooped. "I love it!"

She cheered as a fat man in a pair of shorts and nothing else jumped on a table and began vomiting over those nearby. Cheered even more when a biker wrapped a steel chain around the fat man's skull and dragged him to the floor for a beating. She'd have joined in if I hadn't kept a firm hold on her.

"This is unbelievable," she said, watching a tired stripper blowing a table of Chinese tourists, crawling from one to the other on her hands and knees. "Christ, look at that guy. He's sticking a snake up... Jesus!" Her face paled with shock. Then she started laughing hysterically. Threw her arms around me and hugged hard. "Eyrie Brown, I take it all back. You're a guide of the highest order. First the fights, now this. You should go into tourism. You could charge a fortune to –"

A voice cut her short. Icy and cynical.

"Look what the rats dragged in. Toni fucking Curtis. As if this place wasn't hellish enough already."

Toni stopped dead and I turned to see who was talking. A young woman, maybe a few years older than Toni, was on her feet and grinning viciously. Tall, about five-eleven. Dark hair carefully plastered to her skull to look like a cap, one lock curled under her left eye and stuck to her cheek. Dressed in a red two-piece suit with a yellow shirt. Too classy for a place like this. Obviously slumming it for a giggle. A pair of bodyguards, one on either side. They stood in closer when they saw me looking. Hard faces. Built like wrestlers.

Toni looked around slowly. "Golding Mironova," she cooed. "So this is where the washed-up whores come when they've nowhere else to go."

The other girl didn't flinch at the insult. "This your new fuck?" she asked, nodding in my direction. "You need to be careful," she told me. "That one likes to make men eat her shit and pass it back to her when they kiss. Isn't that right, Toni sweetie?"

"That's what your brother's telling people, so I guess it must be. He should know. Strange thing is, he told me the same thing about you. Said it was the only thing he didn't like about screwing you. Well, that and your liking for dogs."

That wiped the smile off Golding Mironova's face. "You bitch," she snarled and stepped closer. I got between the ladies quickly and held Toni back. Mironova's bodyguards jerked her away from us and squared up to me. One was my size, the other a few inches taller. They looked like they knew what they were doing and I didn't fancy my chances if this kicked off.

"Does Jeb Howard know you're back in London?" Mironova screeched.

"He drove me here himself," Toni sneered, struggling to get clear of my grip.

"Only place Jeb Howard would drive you is to the morgue." Mironova pushed her bodyguards aside and winked at Toni, who was still trying to get past me, wriggling like an eel. "I bet he'd be real interested to hear you're here. Bet he'd pay big for that information, hmm?"

"Be a change, you getting paid for something other than your snatch." But there was a trace of fear in Toni's voice. She was worried. I could sense it and so could Mironova, who smiled lazily and stroked my chin with a long fingernail, never taking her eyes off Toni. I let her scratch and didn't move, my own eyes on the bodyguards.

"I'll be over there for a while," she said softly to Toni, just loud enough to be heard above the noise of the bar, nodding towards a dark, damp corner. (All the corners were dark and damp in DEL'S.) "I never put pleasure before business, even when a bitch like you is involved. If you come over before you leave and offer me a disgusting amount of money – it will need to be *amazingly* disgusting –I'll forget about seeing you and ringing Jeb Howard. Lord knows, you're not the sort of sorry cooze I like having to remember." She blew Toni a kiss. "See you soon, sweetie. And in case you're wondering, I'll want cash. And by the way," she leered, "*love* your hair."

She moved on with a self-satisfied chuckle.

Toni growled, fingers digging into me. There'd be bruises in the morning. "Why didn't you let me at her? I'd have ripped out her eyes and used them as snooker balls."

"What about those two walking wrecking balls she's with?" I said. "You'd have ripped out their eyes too?"

"That's what *you're* being paid for."

"No," I replied. "I'm being paid to help you keep a low profile, not start fights that will draw attention. Besides, it doesn't matter what I'm like with my fists, one doesn't beat two, not when they're built like that. They'd have ground me down and moved on to you."

"We could have handled them," she sulked.

"No," I said again, leading her away. "The first rule of survival – I learnt this long ago, and I'm surprised you haven't yet – is know your limitations. Never take on more than you can handle. If they'd come at us, I'd have fought, and given it my all, but alone, unless I'd got very lucky, I'd have been on a hiding to nothing."

"You weren't alone," she said. "You had me for backup."

I sighed. Mironova and her goons had sat and were sharing a joke. "What gives?" I asked. "Who is she? Who's Jeb Howard? How much trouble are we in?"

"She's nothing," Toni said heatedly, "a jumped-up whore with a –"

"Toni," I snapped. "Don't bullshit me. I can't help you if I don't know what's coming. So tell me, who's Jeb Howard?"

"A gangster like Lewis," she said, pulling a face. "You haven't heard of him? He's pretty big round these parts."

"I told you before, this isn't my game, I don't know the players. Now, if she tells him she saw you, will he come after us?"

"She probably won't be able to tell him," Toni said. "She's not as important as she thinks. A guy like Jeb Howard isn't that easy to get hold of. I doubt she could track him down quickly."

"But if she does?"

Toni shrugged uneasily. "We have history. He took a serious dislike to me some time back, and that was reinforced more recently. If Jeb hears that I'm in town, he'll come hunting and he won't come alone." She looked at me. "Are you known here? If we slipped out, made sure they didn't follow us, could we go back to your place and hole up?"

I shook my head. "I don't come here often, but I'm known. If someone asks questions, it won't be too hard to trace me. Can we buy her off like she said?"

Toni pulled a face. "No chance. That was just her playing with me before she sank in her claws. Even if I paid her – not that I could get my hands on that much cash that quickly – she'd still look to go to him, to drop me in the shit."

"OK. We'll phone Brue."

"No."

"You've got a better idea?"

She chewed her lower lip, genuinely troubled. "We can't ring Lewis. He doesn't want anyone to know I'm in London, but in the event that I'm made, he especially doesn't want anyone to link me to him. He wouldn't help us if we rang. We have to sort this out ourselves."

"You're sure?"

"Call him if you like," she hissed. "You'll just be wasting time. He won't be drawn into something like this."

Toni watched as one of Mironova's bodyguards stood and

headed for the toilet. Her face lit up. "Go after him," she murmured, ducking low.

"The bodyguard?"

"Yeah. Target him in the toilet. Disable him."

"Why? What are you going to do?"

She grew cagey. "Teach that bitch a lesson."

I grabbed her. "What do you mean?"

Toni smiled and picked up her drink. "Toss this in her face. Pull out some of her hair. Throw some slaps her way. Golding Mironova is vain as they come. She likes to think she's tough, but if I knock her about, show her up in front of all these people, she won't go ratting to Jeb Howard. Won't want to admit she was here, for fear he'd find out how I disgraced her in public."

"You're sure?" She sounded confident but I thought it was a weak piece of reasoning.

"You going to sit here arguing and miss your chance, or are you going to go take care of him?"

"What about the other guard?"

"He won't interfere if you're not there, not when it's a catfight between us girls. Go on." She gave me a shove. "Knock him out and come back quick."

I didn't like it but I had to trust her. She knew more about this kind of gig than I did. So I made my way to the toilet.

It was the first time in all my visits that I'd been in there. I'd always held back in DEL'S, waited until I was elsewhere, no matter how full my bladder got. I'd heard tales about the toilets.

It wasn't so bad actually. No worse than any other scummy bar's. A couple of drunks passed-out in the urinals, being pissed on by all and sundry. Puke and shit smeared across the walls. A pimp in one of the cubicles near the back screaming at one of his rent boys, slapping him for refusing to go with a certain client.

The guard was pissing down the parting of an unconscious drunk's hair. He was laughing softly, taking careful aim, leaning forward to watch the urine flow down the man's face. I took out my Hi-Power, reversed the grip, walked up behind the bodyguard and quickly cold-cocked him. Slammed the handle into the back of his neck. Hit him once on his crown as he fell to join the drunk in his own pool of piss. Turned and hurried back to the bar, slipping the gun into its holster. I don't think any of the others even noticed me.

Toni was close to Golding Mironova's table, waiting for me, holding back so that Mironova couldn't see her. I caught her eye. Nodded to let her know it was safe. She smiled victoriously, jaggedly, and I knew instantly that I'd made the wrong call. I cursed myself but it was too late. I'd never catch her in time.

Toni stepped up to the table. Mironova began to laugh, expecting a pay-off. She stopped laughing when Toni pulled her gun, that tiny pistol I should have stripped her of in the apartment.

Toni shot the bodyguard first. Pumped two bullets into his chest as he was fumbling for his own weapon. Screeched merrily as she killed him, then darted after Mironova, who was scrabbling away. Aimed the gun between the shrieking woman's shoulder blades and shot. Mironova stiffened. I was almost on them now. Trying to run. Cutting through the gaps which were opening up as people stepped away from the heat, so that they couldn't be implicated.

Toni's left arm wrapped around Mironova's neck and she rotated her head so they were face to face. I could see the shock and pain in the dying woman's eyes.

"This one's for Jeb, *sweetie*," I heard Toni say.

Then she kissed her foe, biting down hard on Golding Mironova's lips, and fired three more shots into her.

I reached the table and yanked Toni clear. I knew it was too late for Mironova, so I didn't waste any time on her. Began hustling Toni towards the door. She was laughing, Mironova's blood and lipstick smeared across her face.

"You crazy fucking bitch!" I roared.

"Let go!" Toni yelled, producing her knife, another weapon I should have had the foresight to rid her of before letting her step outside with me. "I'm gonna scalp the whore. Laugh at my hair? I'll teach her."

"You'll do nothing. When we get –"

A bullet screamed by my left ear. I threw Toni to the ground and turned, sliding out my gun. The second bodyguard was standing in the toilet doorway, firing. He must have had a far harder skull than I'd imagined to recover so swiftly. Again I cursed myself for not anticipating a potential problem and dealing with it before it could come back to bite me. Should have tied him up, not just assumed he was out of the picture.

The guard would have had us dead to rights if he wasn't still stunned from when I hit him. I returned fire, aiming for his legs, not wanting to go down for murder if the police caught up with me later.

People in the bar were pedalling as far clear of the action as they could get. This was a little too dangerous for their tastes.

Knives and axes were fine, but stray bullets could strike anywhere. Mine hit the wall and door to the left of the guard. Behind me I could hear Toni reloading. Taking her time. Actually whistling while she worked.

A bullet grazed my upper right shoulder. It stung but I knew it wasn't serious. Still, the shock of it encouraged me to aim at the guard's stomach. A long stretch in prison would be bad, but my own death would be worse. If it had to be me or him, I'd make the kill and deal with the consequences later.

Toni got to her knees and rested a hand on my shoulder, taking aim. Fired once and blew half the guard's face away. Put four more into his torso, sending him flying back into the toilets. Stood and puffed on the mouth of the barrel, as if blowing smoke rings away. Smiled and began to say something.

I'd never properly struck a woman before, but I felt I had legitimate reason to break the habit of a lifetime, so I decked her. Knocked her out with one punch. She dropped unconscious and I considered leaving her there. The mental killer didn't deserve to be rescued, not after what she'd done. Three people executed before my eyes. I'd seen hell like this in the desert, but never on my home turf, in such a cold fashion, killed so clinically, so mercilessly, so needlessly.

So neatly.

There'd be every kind of shit I could imagine over this. You could stick a knife in someone, even shoot them somewhere dark and quiet, and not ruffle too many feathers, but you didn't take out three people in a packed bar and walk away without any repercussions.

And I was the one they'd tag. Nobody in DEL'S knew this

girl. (Nobody living, at least.) She was from out of town, an anonymous stranger. Eyric Brown, on the other hand… there were plenty here who knew my face and name and could answer any number of questions about me.

Local kid. Ex-Army. Used to box. Drives a taxi. Lives down Bermondsey way, I think. Nice guy. Hard to believe he got hooked up with a mad bird like that. Did he *kill any of them? I'm not sure, but he was certainly shooting at the guy by the toilet door.*

My only hope was if they didn't talk. And they might not. Folk in DEL'S were usually slow to cooperate with the police. It would become local gossip in no time, and I'd be called in eventually when word trickled through to the investigating officers. But there'd be no proof if nobody volunteered to be a witness, and moral, upstanding citizens were scarce in DEL'S.

If I left her where she lay, the police would take her in and I might get away with it. There'd be no reason for them to look any further. Her gun. Her bullets in the corpses. Witnesses galore who couldn't hide if the assassin was still on the scene when the Old Bill arrived. She could drag me into her mess by naming and shaming me, but I could work with the police, help them build their case against her. Serve a few years, time off for good behaviour, back on the streets in no time.

Except…

One of Lewis Brue's men would be waiting for me. Standing outside the prison gates, grimly smiling. He wouldn't do me there, but he'd follow me, hound me a little, let me think I was escaping, then corner me and let me know he had a present for me from his boss, for a job well screwed.

Cursing, I picked up Toni's limp body and draped her over

my uninjured shoulder. Made for the front door, not running, being careful not to slip. People parted and let me pass, silent, averting their gaze. I could hear the snakes hissing behind their glass barrier, and blood dripping on the grimy tiles. The only sounds in the entire bar apart from my galloping heart.

Outside, the night was cold and the city uncaring. I drew stares as I stumbled to my car, the unconscious girl on my back, Golding Mironova's blood soaked into my shirt and pants, but nobody was keen to stop or question me.

I fumbled for the keys and got the door open after what seemed an eternity. Tossed Toni into the back seat. Took her gun and knife. Wiped the handles clean and stashed them under the dash. Checked my face in the side mirror. Glimpsed at my wound — little more than a scratch, nothing to worry about, wouldn't even need a plaster. Looked around to make sure I wasn't being observed. Sat in. Hit the passenger seat a few times, venting my rage. Started the engine and drove away, leaving the mess, the blood, the witnesses and the bodies behind.

She revived about ten minutes later. Sat up groggy, rubbing her chin. She was lucky I hadn't connected with her nose, or her looks would have been spoiled for life, or at least until she could book an appointment with a very good plastic surgeon.

"What happened?" she groaned.

"I hit you."

Her eyes flared wide. She tried grabbing the back of my head but her hands were slippery with blood and I easily shook her off. "I'll kill you!" she shouted. "I told you I would if you ever hit me again, and now –"

"I could have left you there," I said, busy trying to lose us in the winding back streets of the East End. "Think about that before you fire a few bullets into me. Not that you can fire anything when you don't have a gun."

Her eyes narrowed and she checked to see if it was true. "What did you do with it?" she snarled.

"Left it there with your prints all over it for the Bill to find."

"You didn't," she gasped.

"No?" I looked at her in the mirror. I was mad as hell, but the fear in her eyes mollified me slightly. "No," I admitted. "I should have, and you with it, but sucker that I am, I didn't."

She began feeling her jaw. "You've some punch," she winced. "I'll have to get my teeth checked. I can feel a couple of the lower ones coming loose."

"Get your brain checked while you're at it," I growled.

"Hey," she said, sounding hurt. "What's with the attitude?"

"Fucking hell! You just killed three people. Took out your gun and butchered them. In a public fucking bar."

"Had to be done," she said. "Golding was going to tell Jeb Howard that I'm in London. If she'd done that, we'd be dead. Eliminating her and the guards was our only option. It'll be fine. Nobody else in there knew me."

"What about *me*?" I snapped. "They know *me*."

"Yeah, well, that's what you're getting paid for, isn't it? But you didn't kill anyone. Most they can charge you for is accessory."

"Jesus." I began to laugh, though I felt like crying. "You're some piece of work." I took a sharp left, then slowed down. I'd been speeding. Didn't want to get pulled over. That was the last thing we needed.

I noticed a strange smell. Sniffed the air. It seemed to be coming from inside the car. "You smell that?" I asked.

"What?" She lifted her nose. "Oh." Cleared her throat and grinned oddly. "I, um, kind of lose control when I get excited, and sometimes wet myself a little when I kill someone."

I glanced over my shoulder and saw the damp spot between her legs. "Well, for Christ's sake, don't get it on the seat," I told her, not wanting to have to explain a piss stain to Larry. Then her words sank in. She *sometimes* wet herself *when* she killed someone. That meant she'd done it before, and not just the once.

"How many people have you killed?" I asked sharply.

"That's not a polite question, Eyrie," she reprimanded me.

"Don't play games with me. How many?"

"I don't know. Seven or eight. Maybe more. Sometimes you don't see where all the bullets go."

"Fuck me!" I squeezed my eyes tight for a second and prayed this was a dream. I would have kept them shut longer if I hadn't been driving. "Lewis fucking Brue set me up with a psychopath. That's why he paid so much. Fuck!"

"Chill out, Brown," she said, looking bored. "You keep saying you're not part of my world. Well, this is how it turns. Golding Mironova made a dumb move back there. She shouldn't have let herself be seen. She should have sneaked out, contacted Jeb Howard if she was able to find him, left it at that. In my world, if you make a mistake that big, this is the price you pay.

"You told me about your first rule of survival. Not a bad rule, but I have a different one — *drop the fuckers before they drop you*. Stick with me, kid. You might pick up a thing or two."

I was appalled and awed in equal measures. She wasn't yet

what I'd call a proper adult, but already boasted an ice-hearted outlook that many soldiers who'd seen active duty never developed, and the guts and skill to back it up. I hadn't forgotten how she'd dropped the second guard while my bullets were flying wide.

"What now?" I asked. "Do we ring Brue?"

"Are you a child?" she snorted. "You're being paid to do a job, and this is part of it. Forget Lewis Brue. Take me back to your place. We'll wash off the blood, I'll grab my stuff, and we'll hole up somewhere safe and wait for Sunday."

I nodded slowly. "Brue doesn't need to hear about problems. He expects us to use our initiative and sort things out ourselves. Right?"

She smiled encouragingly. "Now you're getting it."

"Yeah," I replied with a sick laugh. "I'm getting it. It's all becoming clear as a fucking blood diamond."

And I drove.

And I said nothing else.

But in the silence I was thinking furiously.

I parked several streets away from the apartment, in case the car had been spotted and reported to any interested parties. We hurried back to the flat and rushed upstairs. Toni ducked into the bedroom and began looting through her suitcase for a change of clothes. I went slower, searching a drawer for the right lengths of rope — I had plenty from my skipping days as a boxer.

"Do you want to shower first or will I?" she asked, coming out of the room, slipping into a robe. I caught a brief glimpse of her bare breasts but they didn't interest me right then.

She stopped when she saw the ropes in my hands and the look on my face.

"Eyrie?" she asked uncertainly.

"Turn around," I told her.

"What's going on?" Voice starting to rise.

"Turn around."

"Listen, I don't know what you're –"

"I've hit you twice," I said. "The second time harder than the first. I don't think you'd like level three. Turn around." She complied silently. "Hands behind your back." She offered me her wrists. "I'm going to tie you up. Then I'm going to ring Lewis Brue and have him collect you."

"You're a fool, Eyrie Brown," she sneered.

"Maybe. But I'm a live fool and I plan on keeping it that way. Brue told me to ring if anything off the scale happened. Said he'd let me keep the money too, as long as I helped you out of any jam that might arise. Reckon I've done that." I wrapped the rope around her thin wrists and tied a couple of knots that she wouldn't slip out of in a hurry. Gave it a few jerks to be sure.

"Sit down," I said. "Put your feet together. Don't even think about kicking."

She watched as I laced the rope around her ankles. The robe had slid up and I'd have had an uninterrupted view of paradise if I'd been in the mood to glimpse it. But there was nothing on my mind other than phoning Brue and getting shot of her. She was bad news. Fatal.

"Eyrie, listen to me," she said calmly. "You're not acting rationally. That was a sticky situation back there but we got out intact. You did a good job and Lewis will commend you for it.

You might even be able to hit him up for a bonus. But if you quit now, he'll look for the money back, I don't care what he said. Come on. Untie me. Use your head."

I didn't reply. Went to the drawer again. Found masking tape and a clean handkerchief.

"You're going to gag me?" she asked incredulously. "You fucking ape. I can't believe Lewis entrusted me to a chump like you. What sort of a mug panics at the first whiff of danger? You're a –"

I stuffed the gag in her mouth and sealed it in place. Made sure she was able to breathe. Checked the ropes, heedful of circulation. All fine. I could leave her trussed up until morning and she'd be none the worse for wear.

I stripped and showered. Studied my wound in the mirror, but it was as minor as I'd suspected, so I paid it no further mind. Pulled on a fresh shirt and trousers back in my bedroom. Felt miles better. Thought about dunking Toni in a tub of cold water, to clean her up and cool her down, but didn't want her dripping all over the floor.

I made sure I had my phone, then checked Toni one last time before leaving to make the call. Her eyes were wild with rage and hatred, but otherwise she was fine. I kissed my fingers and applied them to her heated forehead. "Back soon," I smiled. "Don't go anywhere while I'm away."

She jerked her body at me as best she could and grunted a curse into the gag. I sighed wearily and locked the door carefully behind me as I went.

SEVEN — A CHANGE OF PLAN

Although I had his number on my mobile, Brue had told me to ring him from a payphone if possible. Although payphones were getting to be relics of the past, there were still a few within walking distance of my apartment. I picked one at random, read his number from my mobile, thumbed in coins and dialled.

Brue had told me I wouldn't get through to him directly, so I wasn't alarmed when a woman answered. I said I was a friend of Stan's (the name he'd told me to use) and had a problem with the flowers he'd sold me. She put me on hold, then I was transferred and a guy asked if the flowers were damaged. I said they were fine but I didn't have a place for them anymore. He asked if that meant I wanted to return them. I told him I did and I was transferred again.

This time Brue answered. He listened silently while I gave him the bare facts. I spoke fast but clearly. Didn't want him to think I was out of control.

"She's in your apartment?" he asked when I finished.

"Yeah. I tied her up."

"Was that necessary?"

"I thought so."

A long silence followed. I could almost hear his brain whirring. He finally said, "Jeb Howard was mentioned, but Golding Mironova didn't have a chance to contact him — is that correct?"

"Correct," I said.

"Good," he sighed. "If Howard was part of this, I'd have to re-evaluate the whole thing, but he wasn't there, his people weren't there, it was just Golding and her two guards who recognised Toni — yes?"

"Yes."

"Then we can forget about Howard, and unless someone else there recognised her, we've nothing to worry about. If you go to ground –"

"I want her off my hands," I interrupted.

Another long silence. I broke it this time.

"You told me."

"Told you what?" Brue replied neutrally.

"That you'd take her back if anything serious happened, assign her to someone better suited to a more delicate situation. I've done my share. I don't want to get in any deeper. Three people are dead, I can be linked, and that's as far as your twenty-five thousand flies with me. Will you stand by your word?"

He said nothing for a few seconds and my fingers tightened on the receiver. Then, to my relief, he came back with, "Like I said when I hired you, I want to do you a favour, not dig a hole for you. I can have a guy at your place in half an hour if that's how you want to play this, but maybe we don't have to go down that route. Can you meet with me first?"

"*Meet* you?" Alarm bells started ringing.

"I'd like to discuss this, try to work things out so it's sweet for both of us."

"Are you setting me up?" I asked softly.

"Is that what you think?" He sounded amused.

"You didn't warn me about Toni. Didn't tell me she was a killer who could fly off the handle in the snap of an eye."

He grunted with exasperation. "I didn't expect her to run

into Golding Mironova and never guessed you'd have to deal with a mess like this. If you want to back out, I'll repeat myself — a guy can be at your place in thirty minutes. But my advice is to come talk with me. If you think I'm setting you up, obviously you'll ignore that and run for the hills, but if you still trust me, if you still believe I'm an appreciative guy who's only trying to return a favour…"

I took a deep breath. It would be easier (*saner*) to wash my hands of this messy business. But Lewis Brue could be a very useful contact if one of the patrons of DEL'S threw me to the police. I might need a friend like him in the not too distant future, if I didn't want to spend the rest of my life in gaol.

Not sure which way to turn, I tossed a mental coin and took a wild chance.

"All right," I said. "I'll come hear you out."

"It's the sensible option," he assured me.

"I'll get Toni and –"

"No need," he interrupted. "She's fine where she is."

I paused. "Are you sure?"

"It will do her good to spend some time trussed up, so that she can dwell upon what she did wrong. Not that killing Mironova *was* wrong – I agree with her that she had no choice in that regard – but she should have taken the business outside the pub and struck in a place without witnesses."

"If someone comes looking for me and finds her…" I said uneasily.

"They won't," he said confidently.

"You can't be sure of that."

"No," he admitted, "but I'm still hoping we can keep this

between you and me. Leaving her tied up isn't ideal, but it's the least complicated course of action. I think she'll be safer there than anywhere else right now."

I would have preferred to take her with me, but he was calling the shots.

"OK," I said. "Tell me where to go."

The first stop was a dark house off the Old Kent Road. Rabbit was waiting for me. He looked like he'd only just woken up. In yesterday's rumpled clothes, which he must have rescued from the laundry. He led me to his car and got in without saying a word. I sat in back.

"Do you want me to wear a blindfold?" I asked.

Rabbit laughed. "You don't have a clue, do you?"

"No," I replied with a grimace.

Rabbit drove carefully, west, finally stopping outside a firm of accountants in Vauxhall. The offices were deserted, not even a security guard on duty, only Lewis Brue, waiting for me in a small room on the first floor, leaning on a desk, chewing a nail thoughtfully.

Brue looked up when Rabbit opened the door and let me in, before closing it behind me and disappearing back to the car.

"Lewis," I greeted him.

"Eyrie," he smiled. "Good to see you again. A little sooner than expected, but we can get over that. I'd like to hear more about what transpired tonight, if that's all right with you."

We sat and I gave him a detailed account. He wanted to know everything, from the moment we'd left my apartment to when we'd returned. He was only interested in Toni, if anyone had spotted her at the fight, if she might have left anything incriminating in DEL'S. It didn't seem to bother him that I could go down for this, but I hadn't expected anything different, so my feelings weren't hurt.

"You're sure she left the pub clean?" he pressed. "No scarf or glasses? A tube of lipstick? A glove?"

"As sure as I can be," I said. "She had very little on her, and we weren't there long enough for her to take anything out of her purse."

"She definitely killed all three of them?"

I smiled tightly. "No doubt about that."

He nodded slowly. "We can only hope that nobody knew who she was, or if they did, that it takes them a while to find out who you are."

"Would this guy Howard definitely target her?" I asked.

"Oh yes," Brue said sombrely. "If he gets wind that she's in London, he'll be on her trail like a hound."

"So why did you ask me not to bring her?" I frown. "If someone in DEL'S ID's me to Howard, and he sends his guys to my flat, and she's there tied up…"

"Then she's dead." He said it without any hint of emotion. "Nothing I can do if that happens. I'm hoping it won't, that you and I can come to an arrangement. If not, I'll ask Rabbit to fetch her when he takes you back. But if Jeb Howard beats you or Rabbit to the punch, she's his and that's that. Toni will understand. She knew the risks when she came here.

"Now, let's assume Jeb Howard *doesn't* turn up. Let's assume she got away from the pub without being tagged. Is there anyone who saw you who'd be keen to shop you in? An enemy or a known grass? Someone eager to make a quick profit by turning you over to Howard or the police?"

I'd thought about this on the way over, so I was able to answer without a pause. "I doubt it. Word will reach the Bill in the end, I'm sure, but I think I'm safe in the short term. I've done nothing to piss off any of the regulars, and grasses know better than to hang out at DEL'S."

"Good," Brue grunted. "That leaves us with options. Here's what I'd like. It's just a suggestion. Please hear me out before making up your mind." I didn't like the sound of that but I held my peace. "I want you to see the job through. Go back and untie her, tell her we've spoken and you're still my man. She'll be furious at you for tying her up, but she's a smart girl and she'll let it go.

"Next you let her wash and dress, then slip out of the flat, get in your car and drive around. Find a cheap hotel, out of the way. Check in under assumed names. Lie low. Come back Sunday as arranged and return her to me. Go home. Wait and see if the police turn up. Play it cool if they do — I'll give you the number of a good lawyer, and pull all the strings I can to make your problems with them go away. When you're in the clear, go buy a boxer and enjoy the rest of your life.

"What do you think?"

I answered immediately. "I think I should transfer your money back to you."

His face darkened. "You think I care about the money?" he barked. "It's yours, no matter what you decide. You kept your end of the bargain. If you want to quit, it won't cost you a penny. I'm just outlining an alternative for you to consider. An extra service, for extra pay, naturally. Say another twenty-five K?"

Another twenty-five thousand pounds...

"No," I said quickly, before I could be tempted.

"Then let's say fifty — no, fuck it, I'm not a cheapskate, we'll call it seventy-five," he said, as if we were talking beer change. "That's on top of the original twenty-five."

My head went into a spin. "That's... you can't be... it's too much..."

Lewis Brue chuckled. "I'd have gone a lot higher than twenty-five if you'd pushed when we were making our first deal — to be honest, I was surprised you didn't negotiate. I'll transfer the money now if you accept."

A hundred thousand pounds. The twenty-five was a game-changer. This... this was so much, it felt like I'd won the Lottery.

I was tempted. It was a straightforward job. Take her to a hotel. Sit tight for a couple of days. Spend the time thinking of ways to spend the money, dreaming about all the things I could do with it.

"No," I said sadly. "Sorry."

"I won't go any higher," he grunted.

"The hundred's enough." I chuckled sickly. "More than. But the stakes are too high. I'm an accomplice to murder. If I cut my ties with Toni now, I might be able to persuade the police that I had nothing to do with her, claim she was a customer who asked me out for a drink, say I knew nothing about her and fled as soon as I realised she was a killer. But if they catch me with her..." I shook my head.

He shrugged. "OK. In your shoes I'd probably do the same. Money's not much good to you in prison, right? I won't ask any more of you. Rabbit will drive you back and bring Toni to me.

That's the last you'll see of us. Keep your mouth shut and your head down and you'll never hear from me again, unless you find yourself in court and need a helping hand — my offer to help you if I can still stands."

"Do you think I should clear out of my apartment, in case Jeb Howard finds out about me and comes looking for her there?" I asked.

"That would be a good idea," he nodded. "The weekend should be long enough. By Monday, if nobody's hit it, you'll be in the clear."

"What about the car I left on the Old Kent Road?"

"Already disposed of."

"I had it on loan from a friend."

He sniffed. "Give me the name of the owner. I'll see him put right, arrange a replacement, call it a bonus for services rendered."

"Thanks." I felt better now. Relieved. It would have been easy for Lewis Brue to fit me up with a pair of concrete shoes, but he was treating me decently. A lot of guys in his position wouldn't have.

"How about a drink before you go?" Lewis asked.

I grinned in response. As if he had to ask!

I sipped the beer leisurely. I'd be glad to see the back of this night, but I was calm now that I'd come through the worst of it. There was still the worry that someone might target me to get to Toni, or that I'd end up doing serious time behind bars, but Lewis Brue thought both scenarios unlikely, and he knew more about this type of business than me. If he wasn't worried, I probably didn't need to worry either.

At least that was what I told myself, and some of the time I almost genuinely believed it. Anyway, if events to come proved me a fool, so be it. I'd gain nothing by working myself up into a panic about the future.

My bladder was bursting, so I asked for directions to the toilet. Stared into the mirror after I'd washed my hands. I'd often wondered what life in the fast lane was like. Now I knew — it was brutal. Reminded me of my time in the desert, but the bloodshed had seemed more natural there, atrocities to be expected in wartime. Brue and his kind were welcome to their world of sudden, extreme violence and casual, meaningless slayings.

I frowned at my reflection. What if he *was* lying, saying what I wanted to hear, tricking me so I'd go back and be a fall guy? I wasn't important. If someone had to be sacrificed, why not a nobody like me? The extra money he'd offered could have been a tease. He might have known I wouldn't take it. A pretence, so I'd think he still wanted me. Maybe Rabbit would put a bullet through the back of my head when we got to the apartment, before whisking Toni away. That would sever the link between myself and Lewis Brue, so that Jeb Howard or someone like him could never trace the trail through me.

I shrugged and tried a weary smile. If it was a trap, I was screwed, simple as that. If Lewis Brue was sending me down, down's where I was going, fast as a bought boxer in the third round.

I returned to the office. Brue was playing with his phone, but he looked up and smiled when I came in, told me to sit.

"I thought I'd get going," I said.

"Are you in a rush?" he asked.

I stiffened and took my seat.

Something in the way I was perched must have tipped him off to what I'd been thinking in the toilet, because he squinted and asked, "Are we good, Eyrie?"

"Fine," I said.

"Still happy with our arrangement?"

"Yeah," I lied.

He sighed. "I'm sorry it went this way, but if I was to do it all again, I'd still come to you first. You held your shit together, protected her, got her out alive. You might be an amateur, but there was nothing amateurish about how you acted tonight."

"Stop," I said. "You're making me blush."

He tapped his phone, then put it away. "Guess you might as well start back. You're obviously not in the mood for a long heart to heart."

"Is that any wonder after what I've been through?" I muttered.

Brue sniffed, a rare flash of irritation piercing his mask. "You'll live." Then he cleared his throat. "Rabbit's downstairs in the car. I've been thinking about how to play this. If we can keep Toni's identity a secret, all the better. I'm going to ring him while you're on your way, tell him he's to stay in the car when he gets to your place and wait for a mystery woman to sit it, then bring her to me here. I'll give her some cash and send her off to find a hotel by herself. I want you to tell her to cover her face with a scarf or something, to keep it covered in the car, and to say nothing to Rabbit on the way."

"I can do that," I said, trying to hide my huge smile of relief. If Rabbit wasn't coming up to my apartment, that meant he wouldn't be shooting me while my back was turned. It looked like Lewis Brue was on the level. My spirits began to lift.

I got up, shook Brue's hand and headed for freedom, a happy man.

Brue stopped me at the door. "I still feel like we're not entirely even – close, but not quite there – so if there's ever any small favour I can do for you, in addition to helping you out with the police if they come knocking on your door…"

"Well, there is one thing," I said.

"Name it," he beamed.

"Never make me an offer like this again."

He laughed. "You don't mean that."

"I mean it," I said coldly, bold now that it looked like he wasn't going to cross me. "You've more than paid off any debt that you felt you owed. The twenty-five K will take me far. Let's leave it at that and part as friends."

Lewis Brue studied me for what felt like a dangerous moment, then nodded benignly. "OK, my *friend*, no more offers. But you know how to contact me. If you ever change your mind…"

"I won't," I said, and then I was out of there, trotting down the stairs, glad to be back in my own world, already thinking about Fervent Eld and making plans.

EIGHT — THAT EMPTY FEELING

The plans evaporated in a heartbeat when I got home and spotted my forced front door, the new lock lying in pieces on the floor.

Stomach shrinking, I pulled my Hi-Power and hurried in, even though time was on my side — Rabbit had parked outside and was waiting, but he'd been told I'd be a while, that the lady would need to shower and change.

A quick sweep of the rooms, leading with the Hi-Power, the way I used to go through a house in the desert, heart pounding the same way it used to pound back then, anticipating the worst possible scenario, no idea who or what might be waiting for me. But the apartment was clear. I relaxed my aim but kept my gun drawn, in case the intruders returned.

One of the ropes was all that remained. It had been severed and tossed aside. I guessed it was the rope that I'd tied round her ankles. Easier to make her walk downstairs rather than carry her.

I pushed the front door closed and took a few shaky breaths. Daggers were stabbing into my brain, and I felt like I was going to faint or be sick.

Toni was gone.

I tried imagining what this would mean. Brue had been dismissive about the possibility of abduction back in the office but I don't think he'd seriously believed she was in danger of being taken. Would he remember that it was his idea to leave her here, that I'd wanted her out ASAP? Or would he invent his own version of the immediate past, where I'd voluntarily abandoned my post and was therefore to blame for her loss?

As I turned in slow, stunned circles, I spotted a note stuck to the TV screen, and my midriff took another blow.

WE KNOW WHO YOU ARE. WE'LL BE BACK FOR YOU.

Neat writing. Block capitals. Black ink.

I didn't know who had left the note, but it looked like they weren't planning to stop with Toni. Or maybe they'd just left it to freak me out. Aim achieved if that was the case.

I came out of orbit and stood weaving by the TV, staring fixedly at the note, thinking frantically, trying to blow away the clouds of fear inside my head, so that I could calmly assess my options.

First option — tell Rabbit she'd been taken. A furious Brue might forget his pledge not to hold me to account if anything bad happened to Toni in my absence. In a rage, he could order Rabbit to shoot me on the spot. He might regret it later, when he'd cooled down, but that wouldn't be any good to me.

Second option — ask Rabbit to take me back to Vauxhall, so I could break the bad news to Lewis Brue face to face. I was sure he'd appreciate the personal touch, but what then? Would he tell me it wasn't my fault and grant me shelter from those who'd said they would return to settle the score with me?

He'd vowed to look out for me if things went wrong, and had given me no cause thus far to doubt his word. But we were into a whole different game here. Brue had been very concerned about the link between himself and Toni, and keeping it secret. If she talked under pressure, there was nothing he could do. But if she didn't crack, that just left me to tie him to her. And his enemies now knew where I lived and had sworn to return for me. In Brue's place, the circumstances being what they were, I wouldn't take any dumb chances. I'd remove the link, no matter how much I might like the guy, no matter what I'd promised him before.

There was also the possibility that Brue might suspect me of being in league with the kidnappers, of taking money from his foes as well as from him, playing the two sides off against one another. I was nowhere near that devious, but the more time he had to think about it, the more his suspicions might blossom.

Third option — I could say nothing, slip out the back and run. But I'd only have a short head start, and Brue would almost definitely then assume that I'd thrown in my lot with the people who'd abducted Toni. I figured it would be easy for him to track me down, but even if I outfoxed my pursuers and laid low for a few weeks or months, what then?

What then?

I found myself peeling the note from the TV and balling it up before I knew for sure what I'd decided. As my trembling fingers crushed it, I nodded slowly to myself. I didn't like the road ahead that I was planning to take, but it was the only way I could see. Glum but resigned, I headed for the front door, throwing the note into a bin as I passed.

Rabbit was waiting in the car, listening to the radio, whistling softly. He looked round with surprise when I opened the passenger door and sat in beside him.

"Where's the girl?" Rabbit asked.

"I've changed my mind," I said.

"What?" he frowned.

"Tell Brue I've decided to go through with it."

His frown deepened. "Through with what?"

"What he wanted me to do. Go back. Tell him I accept his new offer. He's to transfer the money and I'll meet him as and when he suggested."

"What are you talking about?" Rabbit scowled. "The boss told me to pick up a girl. He didn't tell me anything about any other deal."

"If you want to ring him first, fine," I snapped. "I'm happy to wait."

Rabbit shook his head. "I won't discuss something like this over the phone, not unless he's given me clearance in advance and set it up so that he's sure no one is listening in."

I sighed. "I'll come back with you if that's what it takes, but I don't think Brue will thank you for being so thorough."

Rabbit studied me for a moment, mulling it over, then pulled a face. "I don't know what's going on here, but the boss seems to trust you. I'll tell him what you said and leave it at that, unless he gives me follow-up orders."

"He won't," I said confidently and let myself out.

I watched Rabbit pull away and vanish into the night. Then I climbed back up the stairs to the deserted apartment. I looked round once more, in case there were any other notes, then sat on the end of the bed, stared at the space on the wall where the two photos used to hang, and wondered where the hell I was going to go from here.

It was shortly after dawn. I'd called in the gang — Dave, No Nose, Mickey Goodnews, Lucy, Adrian and Caspar. I'd told them it was urgent and they'd all answered the call, no questions asked and hardly any grumbling, even though only a couple of them were early risers and I'd woken the others from their beauty sleep.

A surprised but delighted Lewis Brue had rung earlier, to make sure Rabbit had got it right. Kept the conversation deliberately vague, in case my phone had been compromised. He asked what had changed my mind. I told him I'd thought about my future on the drive back, decided the status quo wasn't for me, that it was time to take a punt and shake up my life. He seemed to buy that. Didn't ask any questions about my *lodger*. Didn't ask to speak with her. Thank Christ.

"You could do with painting your ceiling," Mickey Goodnews told me, coming back from the fridge with a beer. "It's flaking. People are going to see the dust in your hair, assume you have dandruff."

"I think we have more important things to be discussing than the ceiling," No Nose sniffed.

"There's always time to talk DIY," Goodnews demurred.

"Hush, boys," Lucy said softly. She touched my arm and smiled comfortingly. She could see I was wound tight enough to turn a lump of coal into a diamond. "Let's settle down and hear what Eyrie has to say."

What *did* I have to say?

I'd decided to be a hero. Tell Brue nothing about the abduction. Let him think Toni was safe and sound. Try to find out where she was. Go after her. Rescue her. Take her to the meeting on Sunday. Ride away into the sunset with my life and the hundred K. Couldn't be any simpler, right?

Hah.

I knew it was a crazy plan. As if I could find her in a city the size of London. As if I knew where to start or how to look. As if I had any idea how to get her out of the clutches of whatever mad bastard had taken her. I was just a cabbie. Talk about charging at windmills!

But this was my only hope. If I won her back, I'd secure my safety and get out of this mess alive, with a huge wad of cash to boot. If I didn't, I was a dead man. Either Brue would kill me, or the people who'd taken Toni would return and make good on their threat.

(There was one other option. I could turn myself over to the police, tell them everything and take my chances. But I wasn't that dumb or that desperate.)

At least, that was how I saw things. Maybe I was wrong. Maybe Brue would be understanding, and the note was an idle threat. Maybe I had nothing to fear from either set of gangsters. But I couldn't take that chance, and action was preferable to inertia. This way I could at least try to control my destiny.

I looked round at Lucy and the others, who were all staring at me, waiting for me to explain why they'd been summoned.

"I need to find someone," I muttered. "A girl."

"Oh-ho!" Caspar grinned.

Dave groaned. "For *that* I got up at cockcrow?"

"Haven't you heard about Tinder?" Mickey Goodnews asked.

"I think he means a girl that he already knows," Lucy said quietly.

"A girl in trouble," an intuitive No Nose added. "Because I'm sure our good friend here wouldn't call us just to help him find a lady he was sweet on, so that he could seduce her with flowers and chocolates. Am I right, Eyrie Brown?"

"You're right." I licked my lips, working out how much I should tell them. I could trust every one of them but I was determined to be careful. I didn't want them to get too tangled up. This was my mess, not theirs. I'd wanted to keep them completely out of it. That was no longer possible — well, it *was*, but not if I wanted to live too — but I could shield them to some extent, tell them no more than was absolutely necessary.

"Three people were killed in DEL'S last night," I began.

"I heard about that," Caspar piped up. "I was working late. One of my last fares told me. Only he said it was seven or eight who got wiped. Some crazy guy and his foxy lady pulled guns and..."

He stopped, eyes widening into two full moons.

Everybody stared, first at Caspar, then at me.

I coughed discreetly and looked aside.

"Eyrie?" Dave asked quietly.

"I can't tell you who she is," I said. "I can't tell you how I'm involved. All I can say is that I have to find her. I'm a dead man if I don't. I hate having to ask, not least because this could endanger you, but I need your help."

"Is what Caspar says true?" No Nose asked.

"It was three people, not seven or eight."

"You were there?"

"Yeah."

"You killed them?"

"No. It was the girl. She had her reasons. She's connected, know what I mean?" Everyone nodded. "I was supposed to be guarding her, but she's been stolen out from under me. If I don't get her back, I'm going down."

There was silence after that, each of them pondering my words, considering the situation, wondering how dependably boring Eyrie Brown could have got swept up in a tropical shitstorm of this magnitude.

"What do you want us to do?" Lucy eventually asked.

"There'll be talk about the murders," I said. "I want you to listen to the gossip and throw a few apparently innocent questions at those who might be in the know. Nothing obvious. Don't make it seem like you're pumping them for information. I don't want any of this rebounding on you."

"What do you want to know?" No Nose asked.

"Where she is or who might have an idea." I shrugged. "I doubt you'll find out anything definite, but even a sliver of a hint will help. If I know there's talk of a certain gang involved, in the east, north or wherever, I can hit that area and scout around. Right now I haven't a clue where to start. If you can point me towards a whiff of a scent, it'd be something."

"How are we supposed to question them?" Adrian inquired.

"Subtly," I said. "Drop it into conversation casually, like it means nothing. Get talking about the crazy guy and his chick in DEL'S, the way Caspar's fare chatted to him about it last night, the way Caspar brought it up just now. If they respond, act the ghoul and fish for juicy details, as if you're looking for a juicy story to share with your mates. If they don't volunteer information, don't push."

"And if we learn something?" No Nose murmured. "If someone says he knows who the crazy bird was, and suggests he knows a thing or two more, what then?"

"Call me and I'll take the investigation from there."

"This investigation…" No Nose said hesitantly. "I don't want to get involved in anyone's murder…"

"This isn't about revenge," I assured him. "All I want is to save the girl. I might rough up a few people if I have to, but I won't kill anybody, not unless they corner me and I have absolutely no other choice."

They looked around and began to discuss it. I made coffee for them, feeling like an outsider in the gang for the first time ever. They kept shooting me sly glances which they thought I wouldn't spot, like they'd never really seen me before, like I'd changed.

Which I guess I had.

"OK," No Nose said in the end, speaking for the group. "We'll hit the places where there's most likely to be talk about this, bring it up with anyone who might have heard anything, fish for whatever's being openly shared. How long do you want us to keep it up?"

I had to think about that.

"Let's meet this evening at TERRY'S, six or thereabouts if you're OK to work that long. If nobody's heard anything, I'd love if you could try again for a few hours tonight, then again tomorrow morning into early afternoon, however much of that time period you can spare. After that it won't matter."

No Nose nodded, then paused. "Eyrie… if we get a line on whoever took her… if you want some of us to tool up and come with you…"

I smiled thankfully for the offer, but said, "No. I'll take it from there, if we get there. I'm stuck with this craziness but there's no reason why any of you should suffer too. If you find out anything that might help me figure out where she is, or who might know, that'll be enough."

I sipped the coffee and stared into the swirling whirlpool inside the mug. "Hell, that'll be a debt I can never repay," I said softly over the rim, knowing I was asking more of them than a man ever should of his friends, knowing they could get into serious trouble for this, hoping I didn't drop any of them as deep into the shit as I was.

I went to bed soon after they'd left. Had trouble getting to sleep, but slept fairly soundly once I did. Dreamt of beaches and rolling waves. Zahra was in some of the dreams. Toni too. But not together. In my dreams, as in the real world, they were a pair of ladies destined never to meet.

As anxious as I was to start searching for Toni, I needed the rest. I was physically exhausted and emotionally overwrought. If I'd hit the streets first thing and spent the whole day searching, I'd have worked myself into an inert slump by mid-afternoon. I had time on my hands, thirty-plus hours. If I approached this with a focused mind and employed sensible tactics, there was a chance (slim as it was) I might live to see Monday and the week beyond. If I gave in to blind panic, I'd be dead before I started.

I went for a walk when I woke. The exercise helped refresh me. There was a welcome breeze blowing and my head cleared as I breathed rhythmically while I strolled.

Was there any real hope of finding her? Probably not. But there was a chance (again, admittedly, a slim one). News travels fast in London, and nobody has secrets in a taxi — cabbies are blind and deaf as far as our clients are concerned. I'd heard people talking about affairs, burglaries, all sorts of mad shit, without it ever crossing their minds that the driver might be listening and taking note.

That was why Brue had come to me for this job. He didn't want his own men involved. Knew he couldn't trust them to keep the secret. One would whisper it to his wife or lover or best friend. Who'd have another best friend. Who'd mention it to a few acquaintances. One of whom would know a guy who'd pay for such information while it was still piping hot.

He didn't trust me to keep a secret any more than he trusted his own crew, but as had already been many times acknowledged, I wasn't part of their world. My friends were unlikely to mix with their friends. He'd hoped to limit the damage by limiting the circle of people the rumours could ripple through.

After my sleep, I now had only twenty-four hours or so, but I figured there was a chance (I was through quantifying how slim it might be) that someone would talk before the deadline expired. This would be big news, a tied-up killer cleanly taken and carted off into the night. The gossip would surely kick in fast and furious.

Unless she hadn't been kidnapped by someone associated with a gang.

I paused at a zebra crossing as I considered that possibility, which had just struck me. What if Toni's abductor was a run-of-the-mill burglar? He cracks the lock, finds a woman bound up tight, almost flees with fright, thinking he's walked in on some weird sex game. Then he realises she's alone. Mulls it over. Smiles deviously. Frees her feet. Forces her down the stairs and into his car. Takes her home for *entertainment*. Leaves the note to worry me, to make me think it wasn't a random kidnapping.

I could forget the whole thing if that was the case. No way word of something like that would leak, not any time soon. Rapists must, by their damned nature, be better at keeping secrets than the rest of us. He might get drunk one night and boast of the looker he'd swiped, but I'd be long gone by that stage. Dead, on the run or in prison.

I grabbed a sandwich and ate in a park. Sat there munching mechanically and people-watching. Lots of women with kids, and office workers enjoying a break, but I was most drawn to the old men who'd come out to soak up the sun. Would I live to grow tired of life's little monotonies? Would I be sitting here, thirty or forty years from now, remembering this time fondly, as a period of my life when something had actually happened?

I shook myself free of the foolish thoughts. The present was enough to be worrying about. Forget about tomorrow and all its brothers. If I could get through today, I wouldn't be doing too bad.

I bought another lock for the door on the way back. The neighbourhood was busy, as always on a Saturday. Normally I'd be making for the gym by now, if I wasn't there already. Fervent would be wondering why I hadn't turned up. Then again, he'd seen the girl. Had probably come up with a few ideas of his own to explain my absence. Lurid ones, if I knew Fervent Eld.

I fixed the lock when I got home. Don't know why I bothered. I'd have been as well off sticking some tape across the latch. At least then the woodwork wouldn't get chipped every time someone busted in.

Feeling caged inside the flat, I headed to TERRY'S early. Ordered coffee, the pasta of the day and a couple of toasted sandwiches. Wolfed them down. This was going to be a busy night and the last thing I wanted to worry about was a grumbling stomach.

Dave turned up first, fit to drop. I asked why he was so beat and he told me he'd worked a late shift last night and had only got to bed a couple of hours before I rang. I apologised and said I wouldn't have asked him to go out again so soon if I'd known. He waved away my apology and downed his coffee before ordering another.

He hadn't heard anything about the abduction. Plenty of people were talking about the shooting in DEL'S, but nobody was mentioning any names, not mine, not the girl's. Word was it had been a contract killing, two professionals from out of town, long gone before the break of dawn.

"How does it feel, being a contract killer?" he asked.

"You'd better hope nobody ever takes out a contract on *you*," I said and pointed a cocked finger playfully. But he could see I wasn't in the mood for jokes and he didn't say much more after that. He offered to do another shift but I told him to take the night off and get some sleep. It was clear he was wiped. He asked me if I wanted his cab – assumed I'd be doing what he and the others had been up to all day – but I passed. If I was to pinpoint Toni's position and rescue her, at some point this had to go beyond *innocent* questions. Someone would have to not just stick their head above the trench to look around, but leap out and make a dash across no man's land.

That someone had to be me.

There would very likely be severe consequences if I ever got to play my hand, so I didn't want people clocking Dave's cab, or one of my friend Larry's cars if I borrowed another from him, connecting them to me, dragging them even further (and more fatally) into this. I'd find a way to get around. Steal a car if I had to.

Adrian and Caspar arrived next, arguing about the quickest route to Hackney from Morden. The sort of dumb shit the likes of us argue about all the time. They hurried over when they saw me.

"You're in it up to your neck if they catch you," Adrian hissed, sitting down, wasting no time on small talk. "You know who your *girl* shot?" I shook my head, pretending it was news to me. "Golding Mironova."

"So?" I shrugged.

"As in *Smurf* Mironova's sister."

I looked to Caspar, genuinely lost this time. "You know what he's talking about?"

"I do," Caspar said, "but only because Adrian told me."

"Look," Adrian explained. "Smurf Mironova's a mad Russian bastard who... well, he's not actually Russian, it was his old man who emigrated, but he speaks with the accent, you couldn't tell he wasn't Moscow born and bred, unless you were another Russian, then you could probably... Anyway, he's a mad fucker. Has a gang of his own, and they hire themselves out, do the dirty work that other gangs shirk. Cripple innocent people, burn down orphanages, torture kindly old widows, that kind of shit."

I blanched. "And I helped kill his sister?"

"Yeah." Adrian laughed humourlessly. "Word is, Smurf's royally pissed, but it's not just your usual brotherly thing, he seems to have been overly *fond* of his sister, if you follow what I mean."

Caspar's eyes widened. "You didn't tell me *that*."

Adrian shrugged. "That's what they say. Maybe it's the truth, maybe it's bull, but he had feelings for her one way or the other, and he's on the warpath, offering money and favours to anyone with information about the killers, and he's vowed not just to kill the pair when he catches up with them — he's said he's going to make an example of them, the kind of example London's never seen before."

I was growing colder by the second. Like I hadn't enough on my plate, without a psychotic, avenging, incestuous sibling to deal with.

"Has anybody mentioned my name?" I asked quietly.

"No," Adrian said.

Caspar hesitated, then nodded unhappily. "One guy told me about you – he was at DEL'S and saw you – but I think you're safe, far as he's concerned anyway. He's not much of a talker. Only told me because he knows I know you, and I asked him about it, and I think he guessed I already knew you were involved. That said, if he gets wind of the reward being offered by this Smurf guy..."

"Either of you hear anything else?" I asked. "About Toni, where she might be, who might be holding her?"

"Nobody knows," Adrian said. "Least, not that they're saying. There have to be a few more like Caspar's friend who recognised *you*, but they must be keeping it to themselves at the moment, because I didn't hear a word about Eyrie Brown. Not even a whisper."

We drank in silence for a time. I didn't know how to take their reports. Smurf Mironova was obviously bad news, and that meant it was good that nobody seemed to know anything. But if nobody knew or was talking, how was I supposed to find Toni?

Caspar broke the silence. "This Mironova guy. What's with the Smurf business? He a dwarf or something?"

"Nah." Adrian grinned. "It's because of his nose. It's blue."

"You serious?"

"No shit. Blue as the sky. Fucked-up veins or something. Nobody's ever been brave enough to ask. Well, nobody who lived to tell the tale."

The universe being what it is, No Nose arrived while Adrian was talking about Smurf Mironova's nose, so they had to repeat everything they'd told me before we found out if he had anything to share. Turned out he hadn't, except he'd heard my name a couple of times, which was worrying. Once by someone who had been at DEL'S, and once by someone who'd heard a rumour. But neither knew anything more about who the girl was, what it had been about, what might have happened to the killers afterwards.

Adrian left to go back on duty and ask around some more. Caspar had a date that he couldn't get out of. He was very apologetic but said the date had been in place for a long time and the lady had travelled from abroad. It sounded like the makings of a good story, but the story would have to wait for another night. I gave Caspar my blessing and off he trotted, a twinkle in his eye.

Lucy arrived at six-thirty. According to her, my name had as good as been plastered on billboards all over London. Because of her gambling background, she was able to mix with a different crowd to the rest of us, and in those circles nearly everyone knew I'd been involved in the killings. Some were saying I'd shot all three of the victims (or six or eight or ten, depending on the version). Some said I'd been shot myself, an innocent bystander who was only trying to stop the crazy bitch with the gun. Some claimed I was a getaway driver. Some...

The details didn't matter. The city knew I'd been at DEL'S with the killer. Those who didn't know, would soon. Smurf Mironova could be at my apartment right now, waiting, mourning his dead sister in his own peculiar way. I wouldn't let myself worry about that. Not until I had to.

The glamorous female killer was the mystery on everyone's tongue. They figured she was a hired assassin, based on how coolly she'd taken out the victims, and the fact that she'd started shooting first. They thought it was a foe getting back at Smurf, or drug-related — Golding Mironova had been a dealer, apparently, and hadn't been averse to taking her own unwarranted cut of the goods and profits from time to time.

But nobody knew who Toni was. Or that she was still in the city. Or that she had been kidnapped. Or where she might be. On those dark facts the city was silent. Silent as a grave.

Nearly seven. No sign of Mickey Goodnews. No Nose and Lucy had left me to brood alone. Lucy had wanted to stay, but I'd told her I could think more clearly in isolated silence.

I got ready to leave, figuring Mickey was probably glued to a seat at a poker table, blowing his week's wages. I left a tip for the waitress, stood up... then sat again. Mickey was coming in, looking agitated.

He sat across from me. Fidgeted with the sugar bowl that was sitting between us. I could see that he was troubled, so I didn't say anything. Let him get to it in his own time.

"You know about my gambling debts?" he finally asked.

"Yes," I frowned, not sure why he was leading with that. Was he hitting me up for a loan? *Now*, when my life was on the line?

"I'm in deep," he said, gazing down at his hands as I seethed, thinking he was looking to squeeze some cash out of me before someone put me out of action. "My own fault. Everyone warned me. Even the bastards at the track taking my money warned me to quit, told me I was reaching a point of no return. I didn't listen. Convinced I could swing it. One big score and…"

He took out a sugar cube from the bowl, rolled it between his palms, watching it fragment and crumble, until there was a small pile of dust before him.

"My time's almost up," he whispered. "Any day now they'll come for me. I owe too much, to way too many."

"I didn't realise it was that advanced," I said, sympathising with him in spite of my predicament and heated feelings.

"Nobody does. I kept it quiet. Lucy has some idea, but even she doesn't know the full extent of it." He brushed the sugar away and clenched his hands together. "I'm telling you this so you understand. You've been good to me, like the others. You guys have always stood by me, tried to protect me from myself. You…"

He choked up and had to stop for a minute.

"I'm no hero," he started again. "I've always put my own neck first. If this had happened a few months back, I'd have kept my mouth shut and let you burn, because I know I'll burn too if

I get involved. But since I'm dead meat anyway, I might as well go down helping a friend, right?"

I said nothing, staring at him, wondering what he had to say. He looked up and there were tears in his eyes. He blinked them away, dug into a pocket, produced a folded slip of paper, tossed it to me. There was an address on it.

"Ask for Craig Haine," Mickey told me. "He knows what happened to your girl, where she's being held. Maybe she's dead now, or will be before you get to her. I don't know. Ask Craig. He'll tell you, if you force him. He's weak, like me. If you twist his arm hard enough, he'll talk."

I studied the address. Then I looked at Mickey. "I'll keep your name out of it," I promised.

He laughed grimly. "Craig knows I know you, and knows I was asking about the girl. He's no genius, but it won't take him long to add two and two, and there's only one answer." Mickey shrugged. "I don't give a fuck at this stage. If Craig or the guys who took the girl get to me before the loan sharks, good luck to them."

"How much do you owe?" I asked.

"Thirty-five... forty thousand... something like that. Lost count a month or so back. Would have been more except I had a couple of outsiders come in. Pity there weren't a few more like them."

"Mickey..." I took a deep breath, then cleared my throat. "Any chance I could borrow your car? I wasn't going to ask any of you guys – didn't want to get you into trouble – but if things are as bleak as you say..."

"Take it," he sighed. "It's not mine anymore anyway. I lost it a couple of weeks ago. Only reason they haven't claimed it is they're waiting to swoop for the whole lot in one go."

He passed me the keys. I pocketed them, feeling like a rat, but knowing I didn't have time to sit here and comfort Mickey Goodnews.

"Did Craig Haine kidnap her?" I asked.

"No," Mickey said, "but he knows who did and where you can find him."

"Do *you* know?" I pressed.

Mickey was quiet for a few seconds. Then he whispered, "Yeah. Not where the guy stashed her, but I got the name." He began to crush another sugar cube. "Ever heard of a creep called Smurf Mironova?"

NINE — THE JUNKIE AND THE CAT

I rang Lucy as I was driving. Mickey's car didn't have any hands-free devices, and I normally never used my phone when I was behind the wheel, but this was no ordinary day at the office.

Lucy was surprised to hear from me. Thought I was checking to find out if she'd made any progress. Started to tell me she hadn't, but I cut her short.

"You helped Mickey Goodnews out of a hole a while back, didn't you?"

"How do you know about that?" she asked, and I could sense her scowl.

"He let it slip," I lied, not wanting her to know that No Nose had told me late one drunken night when he was raving about what a great woman Lucy was.

"Any business affairs I may or may not have had with Mickey are between me and him," Lucy said icily.

"I agree. But I need to know if you gave him cash or transferred the money electronically."

"Why?" she snapped.

"Because he just got through telling me he's about forty grand in debt."

There was a shocked silence.

"The guys he owes are done waiting," I continued. "They'll come looking for payback soon. From what Mickey said, they won't settle for breaking a few bones. He's history."

"I can't help him," Lucy whispered. "I don't have that sort of money."

"But I do."

Another shocked silence. I let this one ride.

"You'd give that much to Mickey?" Lucy finally asked.

"I owe him," I said.

"He won't learn," she warned me. "He'll gamble himself into this sort of a mess again, the way he always does."

"Doesn't matter," I grunted. "I can help him out this time and I want to."

Lucy laughed. "You're a dark horse, Eyrie Brown."

"Yeah," I smiled. "A pity Mickey doesn't bet on the likes of me every once in a while. So, can you tell me how you paid him?"

"Transfer," she said, which was what I'd been hoping to hear. "Can you text me his bank account details if you still have them?"

"Sure. I'll do that straightaway."

"Thanks. And you can cancel the search. Tell the others they can call it a night too. I have it from here."

"Will do," she said. There was a pause. I thought she was going to ask a few questions or say something mushy, given that we both knew I was heading for a shitload of trouble and this might be the last time we ever got to speak with one another. But then she just said, "Later, Eyrie."

And I replied, "Later, Lucy."

And that was that.

I took a few minutes when I stopped to check Lucy's text and copy the details. Then I logged in to the account that Lewis Brue had set up for me. A quick glance told me he hadn't dawdled — I was now worth a sweet one hundred thousand pounds. I didn't allow myself any time for regrets, just pinged forty K straight to Mickey Goodnews' account and mentally wished him better luck in the future.

I grimaced and muttered, "Mickey fucking Goodnews."

With a self-mocking laugh, I dismissed thoughts of the money and stepped out into the night.

Time to focus.

Walcorde Avenue, off the Walworth Road, should have been a classy affair. A quiet cul-de-sac of old, three-storey, brick houses, situated close to the centre of London. It should have been home to the city's bankers, doctors, stockbrokers. But it had gone awry somewhere along the line and had an unkempt feel to it. A few of the houses looked like they were inhabited by squatters, and among those was the address that Mickey Goodnews had supplied.

The front door with peeling yellow paint was ajar, so I didn't bother knocking.

"Hello?" I called, entering the hallway. "Anyone home?"

A man in his fifties or sixties, in large army boots and nothing else, emerged from one of the rooms. He glanced me over and smiled. "One of Glenn's friends?" he asked bitchily.

"No," I told him. "Looking for Craig Haine."

His nose wrinkled. "No fun in you then." He sighed and returned to his room. Muttered over his shoulder as he went, "Up the stairs. Top floor. The door straight ahead, with the pussy."

I jogged up the stairs. Found a door with a dead cat nailed to it. It was starting to decay, but had been doused in perfume and other scents, so the smell wasn't too overpowering. I knocked, trying not to meet the cat's glazed eyes. There were sounds from inside and, after a while, a thin, squinting guy opened the door.

"Yeah?"

"Craig Haine?"

"Maybe," he said cautiously.

"I want to ask you a few questions."

"You police?"

"No," I smiled. "I'm a taxi driver."

He scratched the inside of his left elbow – scarred from too many needles – and nodded me in. Closed the door after me, having checked to make sure nobody else was lurking outside.

There were no chairs for us to sit on. A single bed with a horribly stained duvet stood next to a window overlooking the road outside. Bare walls, scraps of ancient wallpaper clinging to them in places. Small holes in the uncarpeted floorboards, gnawed by mice or rats. No attempt to decorate or hide the blemishes. A load of empty takeaway cartons in one corner. Nothing of value apart from a laptop that looked top of the range.

Haine sat on the floor by the laptop and pressed PLAY on a film that he was streaming. Christopher Walken started yapping and I recognised it as *King of New York*.

"Good movie," I said, staying on my feet. I didn't want to sit. Afraid a rat might dart out of the shadows and sink its fangs into my arse.

"Seen it three times," Haine said, picking up a slice of cold pizza from a piece of torn cardboard that was serving as a plate. "Walken's gold. Never seen anything with him in it that wasn't worth watching."

I could have argued that – I'd caught him in a piece of crap called *Kangaroo Jack* once – but didn't think this was the time to play devil's advocate.

Haine pulled out a joint and lit up. Didn't offer me a drag, which was fine. I wasn't averse to the occasional puff, but I drew the line at sharing a spliff with a filthy junkie who was almost certainly a walking disease factory.

We watched Christopher Walken dominate the screen for a while. I was anxious to push this forward but figured I'd let Haine finish his smoke. He might be more inclined to open up if he was feeling mellow. I was all for avoiding unpleasantness if possible.

Haine seemed to have forgotten about me until, the joint still going, he turned and blinked. "I don't know you. What do you want?"

I smiled as politely as I could. "I'm looking for Smurf Mironova."

He paused the film and stubbed out the joint. Stared at me more alertly than I'd expected. "Don't know what you're talking about," he snapped.

"Yes you do," I said with a smile that I hoped came across as friendly. "I need to find him. I know you can tell me where he lives, where he hangs out." I forced a chuckle. "Where he takes people he doesn't like."

Haine continued to stare at me coldly. "You want me to set up a meet?"

"No. I'm just looking for an address."

He began scratching his arm again, reddening the flesh, picking at old holes.

"You're a taxi driver?" he asked.

"Yeah."

"You know a guy called Mickey Goodnews?"

I didn't say anything.

"That son of a bitch," he snarled. "You're the fucker who was in DEL'S last night with the trigger-happy she-wolf. The one Smurf –"

He stopped and his arm jerked guiltily.

"The one Smurf...?" I pressed.

"I don't know what that prick Goodnews told you," Haine said, "but he's a headcase. You can't believe anything a loser like that says. He'd tell you the moon's green if he thought there was a score in it for him. I know nothing."

"You know Smurf Mironova."

Haine shrugged. "Who doesn't?"

"You know where I can find him."

"No." His lips went thin. "I did some work for him in the past, but that was a long time ago. I don't know shit. That's the truth. Ask anyone."

I studied his pinched face, thin arms and bloodshot eyes. A sorry, lost cause. Even an amateur like me could see that he would be easy to bully and twist. I was no grand inquisitor – I had a lot of sympathy for people like Craig Haine, knowing that there but for the grace of a few good friends went I – but the situation demanded I adopt that mantle, so I steeled myself for savagery.

"You know about the shooting last night," I said softly.

He shrugged again. "Everyone does."

"You know Smurf found the killer."

"Did he?" Haine sniffed. "First I heard of that."

"You know where he took her," I went on sharply.

"No," Haine whined. "Don't know anything like that. I've been out of those loops for years. That's the truth, man. Swear on my mother's grave."

"Swear on your veins, Craig."

He frowned. "What?"

"Forget it. You admit you heard about the shooting in DEL'S?"

"Yeah," he said uncertainly.

"So you know…" I produced the Hi-Power, "…I'm not a man you fuck with."

His eyes went wide. He started to shiver.

"Tell me what I want to hear or I'll put three bullets in you," I said coldly. "The first in a kneecap, the second in the other kneecap. If you don't crack – and I'm pretty sure you will, given the pain involved – the third goes straight between your eyes and I move on to my next informant."

"I know nothing!" Haine squealed. "I swear I –"

"Craig." I crouched so we were eye-to-eye, not liking what I had to do but determined not to flinch. "Let's not waste each other's time." I pointed the gun. "Which leg do you favour, right or left?"

"Don't!" he screamed, scrabbling backwards. "Don't! I… I'll tell you, all right? If you swear you won't tell him it was me, OK?"

"Talk."

"You won't shoot me when it's over?"

"Depends on what you have for me."

He brushed a trembling arm across his mouth. "Normally I wouldn't have heard anything," he croaked, "but there's a guy, part of Smurf's crew. We're old friends and he likes to shoot up. Smurf doesn't know about that and my friend wants to keep it secret – Smurf pushes his people out to the sidelines if he thinks they're a liability, doesn't take chances on users – so he comes to dealers outside Smurf's regular circle. He visited me this morning, shaking bad, needing the needle. I was able to charge him more than normal, the dumb fuck, he was so –"

"The point, Craig," I growled.

"Yeah. Right. So I prepared the works for him and he shot up here. He got to talking later, when he was coming out of it and in a warm place, started telling me about the crazy shit going on, how Smurf's sister had been killed, how Smurf got the name of a cabbie who was part of it."

Haine started to warm to his story and slipped into the present tense, as if living in the moment that had been shared with him.

"Gary – the guy I know – and a couple of others go with Smurf to kill the cabbie, but instead they find the bitch who'd killed Smurf's sister, tied up in the driver's flat. Smurf starts kicking her so hard that Gary's sure he's going to kick her to death. Gary's thinking it's a pity, wasting a looker like that, but nobody tells Smurf what he should or shouldn't do, so he keeps quiet. Next thing, Smurf stops and smiles. Pulls her to her feet, hauls her down the stairs and bundles her into their car. Says he'll come back for the cabbie, tells one of the boys to leave a message for him, then takes her back to his place, where they can..."

He stopped.

"Go on," I grunted.

"Is the woman something to you?" Haine asked, almost compassionately.

"Never mind that. *Go on.*"

"It's just... I don't want you going mental on me. I'm not part of this. I'm just telling you what I was told."

"Did he kill her?" I asked softly, dreading the answer.

"He might have by now but I doubt it. He wasn't in any rush. Gary…" He wiped his mouth again and picked up the joint. "Gary said the plan was to pull a train on her. Smurf said they were going to invite all their mates round to rape her, let any bugger in London take his turn if he was game. Gary said Smurf was talking about bringing dogs in too – after the rest of them were finished, of course – filming it all, letting her know it was being broadcast, that this would be her legacy, the price she'd pay for having killed his sister. He said they'd fuck her to death and upload it to the web for the world to watch forever."

I stared at Haine, appalled. Toni was a killer who'd done a dumb, savage thing in the pub, but she didn't deserve that. Nobody deserved anything like *that*.

Haine coughed and looked away. "It's a terrible thing, man. I wouldn't wish it on my worst –"

"When were you supposed to take your turn?" I interrupted quietly.

His face turned an even whiter shade. "Me? Hey, not me, I wouldn't –"

"*When*?" I barked, knowing what men like Haine were like, knowing that's the only reason he would have asked for the address, knowing that's why he'd been so eager to share the news with Mickey Goodnews — in case Goodnews wanted in on the action. I didn't blame Mickey for not sharing that with me. I wouldn't have wanted to break it to a friend either.

Haine was trembling wildly now, shaking his head in vehement denial.

"Just tell me," I said calmly. "You haven't gone to Smurf's, so there's no harm done, but I need to know when they were expecting you."

"Later," he mumbled. "Gary said I should wait until there was a crowd, so that Smurf wouldn't spot me. As much as Smurf wants everyone in town to fuck her, there are some people he won't want to see."

A flame of hope flared inside me. "So they haven't started on her yet?"

Haine shrugged. "The plan was to hold tough until all the guests of honour on Smurf's list had gathered, but Gary got out of there quick after they dropped her off. He's nervous. Smurf thinks she acted on her own, just her and the cabbie, but Gary isn't sure. He said it won't surprise him if another gang crashes the party, especially with Smurf issuing an open invitation to rapists of any kind, not hiding the fact that he has her, or even where he's keeping her. He wished me luck if I wanted to take a turn, but he wasn't sticking around for it. I doubt they'll have started, but without Gary there on site, I've no way of checking."

I said nothing for a long time. I was sorely tempted to blow Craig Haine away, but for what? He was a nothing junkie, just keen to cash in on an open offer of a dirty *good time*. There would be dozens, maybe hundreds like him, crawling out of the woodwork in response to Smurf Mironova's seedy summons. If I opened fire and kept going until I'd dealt with all of them, I'd be at it until Christmas next year. Or the year after that.

I stood and put the gun away. "Thank you, Craig. You've been a great help."

"Yeah," he said sulkily. "Whatever."

"I'm going to leave you now," I went on smoothly. "And I

know you're going to keep our little chat to yourself."

"Of course," Haine said quickly. "I won't breathe a word. I don't care about –"

"You're going to keep quiet," I broke in, "because if you tell anyone, Smurf will kill you for telling me about him. Even if you go to Smurf himself, to warn him in person, that won't win you any favours. No one likes a grass, and you've grassed him out big time. If you keep your mouth shut, you'll be fine, but if you talk, the best you can hope for is that he slits your throat. Alternatively, he might throw you to the sickos, the same way he's given them the girl."

Haine flinched at that, but I could see he was on the same wavelength as me. No profit in it for him if he talked. I'd kill Smurf or, more likely, Smurf would kill me, but as long as Craig Haine kept his peace, no one would come to kill *him*.

"Just one more thing," I said.

Haine blinked at me, confused, wondering if maybe I'd changed my mind about letting him live. I squatted beside him and gave one of his thin, spasming knees a squeeze that was half comforting, half threatening.

"Where is she?" I asked.

With a moan of relief, he began to fill me in.

TEN — TOOLING UP

Wallace Keane had served with the Royal Engineers, part of their bomb disposal unit. I had huge respect for those guys. Everyone who sees action in the Forces puts their life on the line for their country and deserves admiration, but those guys have to deal with extraordinary levels of stress. I like to think I had a cool head, but I wouldn't have cut it with the Engineers.

I'd got to know Wallace a little in the desert. He was older than me but we'd come from the same neighbourhood and knew some of the same people. We kept in touch after our respective discharges. Most of my old comrades severed ties with me when I retired early – they viewed me as a quitter for not seeing out my contract – but it didn't matter to Wallace, who'd got out several months before me, having served a lot more time than I had. He allowed me to lean on him for support and guidance when I was back home, made himself available when I most needed a friend who understood some of what I was going through and had an idea of how to best direct me. I thought it strange at the time — we hadn't been *that* close in the desert. Later, when he took me into his confidence, I found out he'd transferred his skills into private enterprise and was hoping I'd go in with him as a partner. I declined – I'd never wanted anything to do with explosives – but we remained friends and stayed in contact, got together every now and then for a few drinks and to reminisce.

Wallace sold his wares to anyone who could meet his price, no questions asked. He had no political opinions or allegiances. In his view, warfare was an economic necessity, and it would be a crime if only our governments and major, established military manufacturers profited from it. He passionately believed that there should be room for the smaller arms dealers too, that crumbs were going to fall from the various tables, and it would be a crying shame if no one was there to sweep them up. Did it disturb him that some of the devices he built were used to kill innocent women and children? Sure. But he was a small fish in a very big pond, his input negligible on a global scale. While he was the first to admit that he didn't make the world a better place, in his view he didn't make much of a negative difference either, so all in all he slept fairly well.

I didn't share Wallace's cynical brand of realism, but I could understand it. His work had never been an issue between us. I had blood on my own hands, and one man's terrorist is another's freedom fighter, so I'd have been a hypocrite if I'd tried to take the moral high ground.

Wallace lived in a rundown, largely deserted, once-industrial area, perfect for his purposes. He was pleasantly surprised to see me when I turned up unannounced and asked for a tour of his yard, though I could tell he knew in an instant that I hadn't come to shoot the breeze.

He'd put on a lot of weight since I'd last seen him, even though it couldn't have been more than a year. A bulging stomach, face lost to layers of fat. He caught me looking while we were walking and laughed. "I drive my doctor mad. He says I'm a heart attack waiting to happen."

"What's behind it?" I asked. "Are you eating more? Exercising less?"

He sniffed. "A bit of both, but mostly it's just old age.

Sometimes time hits quickly and hard, turns you into a broken-down replica of who you used to be, almost before you realise it's happening."

We came to a small shed, one of many in Wallace's maze of a yard, and he pulled out a couple of chairs for us, along with a half-full bottle of tequila, still his favourite tipple after all these years. "So, what are you after?" he asked as he poured a large shot for himself and a smaller glass for me. "I assume it's not to ask about my health."

I told him everything. Wallace Keane was a man accustomed to keeping secrets. His livelihood – his very life – depended on his discretion.

He listened intently as I talked, sipping his tequila, only interrupting a couple of times to seek clarification on minor details. When I finished, he stretched and considered it for a few minutes, his gaze distant, then tossed back the last of his tequila.

"I know Smurf Mironova," he said. "An unpleasant man. A violent, reckless man. A dangerous man."

"You don't think I have a chance?"

He puckered his lips thoughtfully. "I wouldn't say that. He's vicious and fast, hard to stop when he's on the attack, but more of a Tyson than a Muhammad Ali, all brawn, not that much brain. Will he be expecting you?"

"No. To him, I'm just a cabbie." I winced. "Hell, I *am* just a cabbie. No reason he should think I'll come after him. No reason why he'd be frightened if he did."

"And you're truly alone? Nobody at all who could back you up?"

"Not unless you fancy teaming up."

He shook his head. "You know I don't get involved in matters such as these. It'll be tough by yourself. With a few good men you'd have an advantage. A quick assault, create chaos, grab the girl and run while others cover your retreat. As a sole agent... tricky."

"Impossible?"

He hesitated before answering. "If he's keeping her where you've been told, and he doesn't have any special security measures in place... you could very credibly do it. You'll need to be precise. Swift. Can't afford any mistakes. And you'll need luck. But yes, it can be done."

I started to smile, but he raised a finger to stop me.

"Two questions you should ask yourself before you commit," he said. "One, do you think there's a genuine chance that she's still alive? And two, even if she is, do you think she'll want to live after something like that, assuming Smurf and his crew have already gone to work on her?"

I flinched, trying not to picture Toni surrounded by a gang of eager rapists.

"I've got to hope they haven't set about her yet," I said.

Wallace raised an eyebrow.

"I know," I groaned. "Hope is a fool's banquet, and the fools who sit down to dine on it usually die of starvation. If I knew for sure that they'd started, that she'd been destroyed, that she was lying there praying for death, it might be different. But from what the junkie told me, they really might not have gone into action yet. If they haven't, the saving will be a *true* saving."

Wallace sighed. "I can't tell you what to do. It's your show. Me, I'd get out of town, hit the bottle hard, try to forget all about it."

"I can't do that," I said.

"Too noble?" he asked.

"Too stupid," I grinned.

Wallace laughed. "Are you going to drink that or not?" he asked, nodding at the tequila, which I hadn't touched.

"Not tonight. I need to keep a clear head."

"Waste is a sin," he said, picking up the glass and finishing it off himself. "So, how can I help?"

I shuffled forward. "Two things. First I want to discuss my plan with you. Tell you what I'm thinking. See if you've anything to add or suggest."

"No problem. Glad to help. And second?"

"Second," I smiled tightly, "I want to buy some gear."

Wallace half-heartedly approved of my plan. Thought it was the best I could come up with, given the circumstances. "I'm not saying it'll work," he stressed, "but the way things are, working solo and with time against you, it'll have to suffice."

He recommended I keep things simple on the equipment front, some Semtex and basic timers. Took me to another shed where he began unpacking the materials and organising them.

"We'll set the timers here and number the blocks before you leave," he said. "It's straightforward enough, but you'd be amazed how easy it is for an amateur to fuck it up. The first few will detonate together. The rest will go off one after the other, every thirty or so seconds, for about five minutes. That enough time?"

"Should be. I'm screwed if it's not."

"Catch!" He tossed me a slab of Semtex, trying to frighten me, but I wasn't *that* ignorant. I knew it was safe in this state, so I caught it and lobbed it back at him like a cricket ball. He kissed it, then grew serious. "Let's say you get in. Stick the explosives in place, behind machines or under tables, priming them as you go. Most important thing is to make sure you lay them in the right order. You don't want number six going off before number one."

"I'm not that dense," I growled.

"Even the smartest of us can make the simplest of mistakes," he warned me. "Don't get cocky. Double-check at every step. When you've set them all, note the time, sit back and wait, then make your move at exactly the right moment."

"You'll synchronise the timers with my watch?" I asked.

"Of course. And I'll give you a spare watch too, in case yours breaks — don't smile, that sort of thing happens all the time."

I stared at the soft material in Wallace's hands. It always amazed me how something so innocent-looking could be so destructive.

"Nobody gets killed?" I asked softly.

He shrugged.

"Wallace..." I growled.

"I'm not going to make any promises," he said. "They're minor charges, enough to blow up the machines, turn the tables over, give people a scare. But there will almost certainly be injuries — flying glass, metal, wood. I can't say for sure that a shard of glass won't jab through someone's eye and pierce their brain. I can't say with certainty that there won't be a guy poking round the back of a machine when it goes off."

He registered my look of unease and offered a supportive smile. "While I can't make any guarantees, I'll be very surprised if there are fatalities. As long as you get the order right, and set them far enough apart, they should shake the place up, nothing more."

I felt very mixed about this and would be sickened if I walked away with the blood of innocents on my hands.

Then again, how many innocents turn up for a non-consensual gang bang?

"How much do I owe you?" I asked.

"Give me a minute," Wallace muttered, pulling out a piece of paper and a pen. He began scribbling quickly, finished in seconds and handed me an itemised bill.

My eyebrows lifted. "I thought you'd tell me it was on the house. A gift from one old pal to another."

"In your dreams," he snorted.

"Want me to transfer the money now?"

"Well, given that you probably won't be around to do it Monday..."

I laughed and used my phone to log in to the Lewis Brue account again. The way the night was going, there wouldn't be much of it left by the time I was done, but that was far from a worry right then.

Wallace prepared and numbered the bombs, synced the timers with my watch and the spare, which I slipped onto my other wrist. He checked everything one last time, then zipped the goods into a canvas bag.

"My role in this is ended," he said as he passed me the bag. "All that I can do now is wish you all the luck in the world."

"Do you think I'll need it?" I asked.

"You and me both, my friend," he sighed, patting his oversized stomach.

Wallace led me back to the gates, shook my hand and bid me farewell. He didn't say anything corny, like *Take care, buddy* or *Make sure I see you later, OK?* That sort of claptrap was for the movies.

I put the bag in the trunk of Mickey's car, then got in and started the engine. Drove away without looking back, fully focused on the task that lay dead ahead.

Time to dance with the devils and hope I didn't get burned.

ELEVEN — INFILTRATION

The casino was a low-key, grungy affair set in a converted warehouse on the outskirts of Shoreditch, as few lights as they could get away with, no neon signs, little to draw your attention to the place. I'd passed it in my cab a few times over the years but never taken much notice. The gamblers hadn't taken much notice of me either — the clientele in this sort of shoddy establishment rarely bothered with black cabs, unless it was to deface them and steal their wheels. Mickey Goodnews had probably whiled away a lot of hours here, as it was built to appeal only to the most pitiful, hardcore gambler.

I parked round the side, outside a perimeter wall, near a small steel gate that Haine had told me about. A couple of scummy figures were watching porn on their phones. They eyed me closely as I got out, wary of anyone who wasn't a regular. I ignored them and made my way to the door at the front of the building. They didn't challenge me. Figured I was here for the Toni Curtis show. Which I was, just not in the way everybody else was.

There used to be a name over the door but it had fallen off or been dismantled a long time ago. Craig Haine had referred to it simply as SMURF'S PLACE. An ancient, weathered sign on the wall read NO UNDER 18s. Maybe the bouncers were illiterate, because they let through a couple of kids ahead of me who couldn't have been more then fifteen.

The two thugs in cheap suits glared at me as I approached. I wasn't their usual customer, and would have warranted closer attention another time, but I was sure they'd seen a lot of unfamiliar faces tonight.

"All right?" one of them grunted.

"Yeah," I grunted back.

"Haven't seen you here before," he said.

I forced a leering smile. "I'm here for the special." That was the code phrase that Haine had shared with me.

The guard returned the smile. "Have fun."

And I was in.

The teenagers who'd preceded me weren't alone in the crowd. At a guess I'd have said at least half of the jackals roaming the aisles would have had trouble convincing a cinema usher that they were eighteen. This was a popular spot with the local *yoofs*.

The others were a miserable mix of no-hopers, many middle-aged or older, wearily feeding coins into the battered slot machines. They never smiled, even when they won, just went on rolling in the coins, like assembly line robots.

I walked past the first few rows of slots. Video games were mixed in with them, and these were popular with the pimply teenagers smoking joints and swigging cheap beer that they'd probably swiped from a supermarket. (I'd never understand why they didn't steal the good stuff.)

The lights were dim, the music loud. Harsh, pounding tunes, some kind of heavy hip-hop that seemed to be all the rage. The kids liked it, banged their heads, did a few jerky dance moves. The older customers blanked it, deaf to the sounds, immersed in their own little worlds.

The machines made a music of their own. Buzzers and bells, falling coins and sirens, shouts and cheers, zaps from futuristic lasers. I recognised the sound of a Space Invaders game and looked round to see an old lady in a pair of slippers, all by herself, fighting to save her planet from the green alien menace.

I had to smile. This was like being in a time warp. The grotty cave was more of a 1980s amusement arcade than a twenty-first century casino. Give it another few decades and archaeologists would be swarming around, digging up clues to what life was like back in the Thatcher and shoulder pads years. The old dear in the slippers would probably still be here, driving back the Invaders.

I completed a full circuit a couple of times, getting to know the place, choosing my spots. It was larger than I'd imagined, row after row of machines. There were a few roulette wheels and craps tables, but most of them were covered in plastic, and croupiers were thin on the ground. Smurf Mironova had no interest in trying to run this as a proper casino. It suited him fine the way it was.

I noticed a couple of hard nuts circling as I was, and wondered if their job was to deal with possible Toni-related threats. But then I saw them having a quiet word with a guy who was leading a few teenagers to the toilets, and realised they were merely on the lookout for dealers. Drug deals were apparently condoned in the casino, but seemingly only from approved sources, I guess to ensure that a fair chunk of the proceeds wound their way back to Smurf and his team.

The guards were suspicious of me at first, with the bag over my shoulder, but relaxed when they saw I wasn't approaching the gamblers. They should have quizzed me regardless, but as Wallace had guessed, security here wasn't as tight as it should have been. Besides, this wasn't a normal night, and I wasn't the only unfamiliar face roaming the aisles, taking a curious tour of the dive before heading through for the main attraction.

There was an exit at the rear of the building, blocked by three men who were almost double the size of the guys on the front door. Haine had told me there was a yard out back, with a tall, narrow building on the opposite side, a hangout for Smurf and his crew. That was my ultimate destination, but not quite yet.

I checked my watches. Time to start setting the charges. It was almost too easy. All that noise, all those bodies, all the dark spaces that had been purposely created for shady deals and quick screws. I could have planted twice as many devices as I was carrying and nobody would have been any the wiser.

Wanting to avoid a body count, I carefully targeted the quieter areas, the less popular machines and inactive, dust-swamped gambling tables. Ducked out of view – not that anyone was watching – reached into the bag, unwrapped a package, slapped the Semtex in place, walked away. Simple as that.

When the bag was empty, I studied the watches, waited until it was almost time for the fireworks, then pulled out the baggy cap that Wallace had given me. His idea about how I could sneak my gun past the guards. I'd taken out the Hi-Power earlier, dropped it into the cap and stuck it in place with tape. Now I jammed the cap on my head. Wallace said it was the oldest trick in the book, yet still worked when you were dealing with the cut-price characters that Smurf Mironova liked to surround himself with.

I ditched the bag and made my way to the rear exit. The guards bunched together to block my path as I approached, but relaxed when I told them I was here for the special.

"Good job you didn't leave it any later," one of them growled. "You might have missed all the fun."

"Have they started already?" I asked, trying to sound casual.

"Not sure," he said. "Don't think so, but we've been on duty here for hours."

"Gotta check you before we let you through," one of the other guards said. "No weapons allowed."

"Of course." I put my palms against the wall and let him frisk me. He did a lame job of it. In retrospect I could have just stuck the gun down the front of my trousers.

"He's clean," the guard said, and the last of the Three Wise Men opened the door and walked me through. The door closed after us and I was in the open yard with the guard, in the welcome night air.

"You coming too?" I asked as he nodded me forward and followed.

"Just showing you the way," he said. "Everyone gets an escort."

"What's your name?" I asked.

He looked surprised by the question, but answered, "They call me Spursy."

"You a big Spurs fan?" I smiled.

"No," he snarled. "Hate them."

"Bit of an unfortunate nickname then," I noted.

"Only unfortunate for those who laugh at it," he said.

I paused and looked round the yard. "A bit of a hole, isn't it?"

The guard shrugged. "Perfect for what's going down tonight."

"Worked here long?" I was desperate to make small talk and slow things down, not wanting to get to the building at the far side of the yard before the first of the devices went off.

"A couple of years," the guard sniffed, happy to chat. "Don't just work in this place though. I get around, do all sorts of — *Jesus fuck!*"

He ducked instinctively as the retort of the first explosive roared through the night. I ducked with him, yanked off my cap, grabbed the gun and ripped it free.

"What's that?" I screamed, acting scared, keeping the gun hidden down by my side, not wanting to use it unless I had to.

The guard didn't answer. His jaw was hanging low. He was staring back at the casino, though we couldn't see anything from out here.

"What's happening?" I shouted.

The guard reacted this time. Rose swiftly and cracked his knuckles, looking excited to finally be dealing with something other than unruly teenagers. "Stay here," he barked, and set off back the way he'd come.

Ignoring the command, I moved quickly in the opposite direction to the guard, heading straight to the small building that had been my destination since my date with Craig Haine earlier in the night. I hammered wildly on the door, yelling as if panicked, and it opened within seconds. A couple of men spilled out, guns in hand.

"What the fuck are you up to?" one snapped.

"Somebody's blowing up the casino!" I screeched as the screams from inside echoed our way. Another device went off. They hadn't heard the first explosion, but they heard this one and flinched with shock. "One of the guards got hit!" I panted, even though that made no sense, given that the bomb had gone off inside the casino and we were out in the yard. "I think he's dead!"

"Fuck!" the guys yelled and rushed towards the casino, where they banged on the door, then forced it open when nobody answered.

More people were emerging from the small, narrow building. Angry men and curious women, Smurf Mironova's inner circle, spilling out to see what the fuss was. I noticed one guy with a blue nose — the low and mighty Smurf himself. I gently pushed against the flow, heading into the building while the others were streaming out. Nobody paid me any notice. They were transfixed by the casino, staring with uneasy awe at the smoke and flames that they could see flickering through the open exit door.

This was what I had planned for, but I hadn't truly believed it would pan out this way. Muting my delight – mindful of Wallace's warning not to get cocky – I hurried in past the last of the stragglers, knowing the confusion wouldn't last. Smurf and the others would return. I had to work fast.

I checked all the rooms on the ground level. No sign of Toni. Hustled up the stairs. I wanted to shout but restrained myself. The less noise I made, the better. Began going through the rooms on the first floor, when I suddenly heard someone shouting.

"Come on! Fuck's sake! We're missing it all!"

I moved ahead cautiously as another voice cried out, "Wait a minute! I'm not leaving till I've shot my load."

"Hurry, Harry," the first guy said. "Someone's torched the arcade. If Smurf finds out we stayed behind, he'll..."

There was an open door ahead of me. The guy who was speaking was shuffling through, pulling up his trousers, dick still half-hard. Noticed me just before I clubbed him with the gun. Managed to half-duck, avoiding the worst of the blow, so I had to strike again. This time he didn't get up.

I entered the room. It stank of sweat, beer, dope. Toni was tied to a mattress on the floor. Naked, still stained with dried blood from DEL'S. Plenty of fresh blood too though, cut and bitten in many places. Streaks of sperm across her stomach, breasts and face, that beautiful face distorted with hatred, fury, desperation.

She saw me past the arse of a man who was standing next to her, masturbating savagely. He was fixated on Toni, oblivious to my presence. Toni's eyes widened. She started struggling and grunted into the gag. The masturbator whooped. "Don't worry, little lady," he cackled. "It's coming soon. A taste of what's in store for you when I come back for the *real* party. Let's see if I can hit an ear..."

I marched up behind him, grabbed his hair, jerked him around and smashed his face with the butt of the gun. Then I dropped the gun and laid into him with my fists, cursing and spitting as I pounded him, wanting to smash through to brain and still not stop.

Then I remembered the timers, and Smurf and his men, and I let the creep drop. No time for losers like him. I had to get Toni out of here before her tormentors returned en masse.

Toni's knife was lying nearby in a pool of blood. I picked it up and bent to free her. I thought they'd just lightly sliced her with the blade until I started cutting the ropes around her wrists.

I stopped, horrified, when I saw that they'd hacked off the tips of her two little fingers.

I felt my hands shaking, but I hadn't time for an emotional breakdown, so I put the torture from my mind and quickly cut through the last of the ropes. Ripped off the gag, absently (and sickly) noting that it was the one I'd stuck in place myself. Smurf must have been saving her screams for later.

Toni couldn't make any sort of noise apart from a low mournful dirge. I picked her up, cradled her in my arms like Mary holding Christ in a pietà, and let her face press into my chest.

"I'm sorry," I whispered.

"They c-cut off my…"

She held up her left hand.

"I know. I'm sorry. Did they…?" I left the awful question hanging.

"No." She managed a sick chuckle. "Stupid fuckers couldn't even get that right. Smurf would only let them play with me. Waiting for some Russian friends of his. He'd promised them first dibs." She looked at me, smile fading, tears forming, and croaked, "You came to rescue me."

"Save the waterworks for later," I grunted. "We have to get out. Now. While we have a chance. Are you ready?"

She scowled and cleared her throat. Wiped a bloodied hand hard across her cheeks to drive back the tears. Whispered gruffly, "Clothes?"

"No time." Still holding her naked body in my arms, I started out the door and down the stairs. "When we get away, we'll find clothes for you and get you to a doctor. But first we've got to get away."

"*Smurf.*" She said his name clearly, through gritted teeth.

Again I said, "No time."

I crashed through the open door at the bottom of the stairs. A woman in a robe with a strap-on dildo poking through was standing nearby — it looked like some of Smurf's female friends had planned to get in on the action too. She saw us and began screaming. One of Smurf's men turned towards me, pulling a gun. I fumbled for my weapon but it wasn't there. I'd only fucking left it upstairs after tending to the imprisoned Toni.

I swivelled, hoping to shield Toni, knowing it was a futile gesture, that we were both screwed, when there was a blast directly beside my ear. I winced, then looked round, surprised not to feel any pain — the guy surely couldn't have missed from that close.

What I saw didn't make sense. The man was lying on the ground, his head a shattered cathedral of blood and exposed bone.

There was another blast and the chest of the woman in the robe blew open.

I looked at Toni, stunned. She had my gun and there was death in her eyes. "Put me down," she hissed. "I'll kill the fucking lot of them."

I began running for the gate that Craig Haine had told me about, the gate in the yard, the gate I'd deliberately parked near when I arrived.

"Eyrie!" Toni screeched, shooting at the crowd outside the casino, hitting a couple of random people. "Put me down!"

"We're getting out of here," I gasped, seeing the gate get nearer.

"No! I'm staying! I want to –"

"There's too many!" I shouted. "We have to get out while we can. We're alone, Toni."

She fell silent but kept firing. More people were starting to notice us, but they couldn't chase while she had them in her sights. A couple tried and paid the price. Her ordeal hadn't affected her aim — every bullet she fired found its mark.

We reached the gate. It was secured with a lock and chain. No sign of a key.

"I need the gun," I huffed.

Toni ignored me and looked for another target.

I put her down – but kept a firm hold on her – and said again, steadily this time, "Toni, I need the gun. We can't get out otherwise."

She glanced at me, eyes afire, then down at the lock. She twisted slightly, took aim and shot the lock to pieces. Turned back and fired another shot at those in the crowd.

I took a chance, released her – I was relieved when she didn't run straight back towards the crowd – kicked the lock clear and began unwinding the chain.

A regular Hi-Power magazine holds thirteen 9mm bullets. More than adequate for most occasions that it will see use, but nowhere near enough this time. Toni ran dry.

"I need another clip," she shouted.

"Give me the gun," I yelled, reaching for it.

"A clip," she snapped, keeping it out of my reach.

I had no choice but to hand her a fresh magazine. She wasted no time and had already reloaded and opened fire again by the time I tossed the chain aside and pushed open the gate.

The two guards in the alley outside – I'd forgotten about them in all the excitement – had pocketed their phones and drawn their weapons. They fired as soon as they saw me, which was a mistake — they should have let me step all the way through.

I ducked back just in time to avoid the bullets, which struck the brick wall and steel gate, which swung closed once more.

"Toni!" I yelped. She spun, moved forward, kicked the gate open again and began firing at the guards, ignoring their own shots, acting like her nakedness was an impenetrable shield.

Five seconds later there were two steaming corpses lying on the alley floor.

We limped through. I paused to push in the gate, to provide us with cover, and saw that some of the men from the crowd had broken free and were giving chase. I picked up Toni again – the yard was full of stones and broken glass, and her feet had been cut – and hauled her to the car, ignoring her protests, letting her carry on firing. I laid her across the bonnet while I rooted in my pocket for the keys and opened the door. I heard more gunfire but didn't look round.

I turned to get Toni but she wasn't there.

She was striding back towards the gate, leaving bloody footprints as she moved at a surprising speed. I chased after her but she was too far ahead. Then I saw where she was headed. Not back into the yard, as I'd first thought. One of the men who'd chased us was down but not dead. He had a blue nose and he was her target.

"Toni!" I yelled, trying to stop her.

"Stay back, Eyrie," she warned. "If you try to stop me, I'll kill you."

I came to a halt. She meant it, regardless of what I'd done for her. She had her chief tormentor in her sights and nothing was going to get in her way.

I hovered, unsure whether I should stay to see what happened or get out while I could. Decided since I'd come this far, I might as well see it through.

Toni paused by the gate and addressed those still in the yard. "I'm Toni Curtis," she shouted, voice incredibly firm. "I've been tortured and disgraced, and you sons of whores were going to rape me to death once you'd been given the green light."

I could hear the noise in the yard dying down, people stopping to listen, awed and fascinated. They heavily outnumbered her. If they'd attacked as a group, she could have done little to repel them. But her voice made them forget their superior numbers and held them in check.

"If I had my way, I'd kill every single one of you fuckers," Toni went on, "but I don't have the time or the bullets. What I do have is Smurf Mironova. I'm going to execute him where he lays, mewling like a newborn calf in his own blood and piss, and if anyone interferes, you'll get the same. You hear me?"

She screamed her challenge, which went unanswered, then sauntered over to the stricken Smurf. I couldn't see what was happening on the other side of the wall, but nobody shot at her and nobody came near the open gate, even when her back was turned to it.

Smurf was trying to drag himself to safety. He'd been shot through the stomach and was suffering. I could feel Toni's dreadful smile igniting the night. And I have to admit, I smiled with her.

She stood over Smurf, used one of her bloodstained feet to turn him over onto his back, took aim and blew his cock and balls to nothing.

He screamed. As you would.

Toni shuffled forward, so she was over his face. He could have grabbed her legs and wrestled her to the ground, but he had grabbed his ruined crotch and couldn't let go.

She crouched on top of him. For a moment I thought she was going to make Smurf Mironova perform a sex act on her. But then she brought the gun up and stuck it in his mouth. I saw a thin stream of urine hit his chest, and remembered what she'd told me before, about what happened when she got excited. When she killed.

Toni took the gun out of Smurf's mouth, put it under his blue nose, and shot it off. His screams hit an even higher notch, and didn't stop until she jammed the barrel into the space where his nose had been and shot twice, turning his brains into pizza sauce.

She stood, stooped to collect something, then started back towards me. Collapsed after a few tottering steps. I hurried forward, picked her up and ran with her to the car. She was still clutching the gun. I took it from her, fired the last few bullets at the gate – I could hear those inside the yard starting to edge towards it, getting their courage back – then shoved her inside the car, jumped in after her, turned the key and jammed my foot down.

And we were gone.

Alive.

Triumphant.

I looked at the stricken girl beside me.

Hurt.

TWELVE — RECUPERATION

Toni sat, crouched into a ball, trying to hide her nakedness. Her eyes were steady and centred on something beyond the range of vision. She hadn't said anything since she'd finished with Smurf and returned to the car. I was too busy driving to try to comfort her. We had to put some serious distance between ourselves and the scene of the carnage.

"Smurf kept telling me what was going to happen," she said softly, not looking at me. "All the crazies he'd invited, all the things they were going to do to me."

"I'm sorry it took me so long to find you," I said.

"He told me they were going to film it," she said, giving no sign that she'd heard me. "Make me watch it over and over before they killed me, then upload it to the internet. My memorial for all time."

"You're safe now," I muttered.

She didn't reply. Then, a few minutes later, she giggled hoarsely.

"I took a souvenir."

She held out her left hand, which was curled into a fist. Opened it. I glanced down and saw something blue. Took me a few seconds to clock what it was.

"Christ!"

She raised the remains of the nose and held it over her own. Then she began to sing. *"Mironova, the blue-nosed reindeer, had a very..."*

She stopped, choked on a laugh, and started to cry. And once she'd started, I knew it was going to be a long time before she stopped.

Saying nothing, keeping my gaze on the road, I did what I did best.

I drove.

Although I hated having to involve her, I took Toni to Lucy's. I wanted to keep my friends as distanced from the fallout of what had happened at the casino as I could, and would have preferred not to drag Lucy into this, even in the most minor way, but I needed clothes for the naked young woman in the car.

I parked as close to Lucy's apartment as I dared and told Toni where I was going. She didn't want to be left alone, but I couldn't take her outside, not naked like she was. She agreed to remain behind, but reluctantly.

"Eyrie?" she whispered as I was getting out.

"Yeah?" I looked back.

"Don't be too long. Please."

Her fingers were clenched and she was trembling. So unlike the brash, overly confident stunner who had come to my apartment just two nights earlier. I didn't think Smurf and his creeps had broken her, but they'd certainly pushed her close to the point of breaking. If I'd been just a few hours later... if those Russian friends of Smurf's had got to her before me...

"I'll be fast as I can," I promised, and ran for the door.

I had to ring the bell several times before I got a response. Finally a heavy-lidded Lucy answered, blinking in the light. "Eyrie?"

"Hi," I panted. "Can I come in?"

"What time is it?"

I checked one of my watches and was surprised by the advanced hour.

"Gone three," I told her. "But it's important." Thinking of what Toni had said, I added, "I won't keep you long."

Lucy hesitated, then unlatched the door and let me in.

"What is it?" she asked.

"I need clothes. A couple of dresses. A few tops. Underwear." She was a little larger than Toni, but close enough.

Lucy gawped at me like I was mad. Then understanding dawned. "The girl?" she asked softly.

I nodded.

"What –" Lucy started to ask.

"Please," I stopped her. "Don't ask any questions. I don't want to put you in a compromising position." Knowing Lucy would make me bring Toni inside if I told her what had happened, that she'd insist on helping.

Lucy stared at me uneasily, then decided to honour my wishes. "Wait a sec." She headed for the bedroom, taking care that I couldn't see inside. I didn't have to. I'd spotted No Nose's car outside. If the moment hadn't been so critical, I'd have smiled.

She returned with her arms full of clothes. Much more than I'd asked for or needed. She spread the load on the couch and I went through it, picking out bits and pieces, mostly dark wear.

"How about bandages?" I asked.

"Sure. Anything else?"

"Antiseptic? Some swabs?"

"Coming right up."

While she was fetching medical supplies, I folded the clothes neatly and made a tidy pile of them. I was an expert at folding after my years in the Army. A habit I'd never outgrown.

Lucy returned and handed me a small bag.

"I packed some extra stuff," she said. "Painkillers. A needle and thread. Other bits and pieces that might come in handy."

"Thanks." I kissed her cheek and turned to go.

"Eyrie," she stopped me. "Will you be back?"

I'd been wondering that myself. Smurf's people would surely assume that Toni's rescuer was the man they'd kidnapped her from, but would they bother to come after me now that their leader was dead? Perhaps his replacement would want to put the past behind him, wouldn't care about the Mironova executions as long as I wasn't a threat to him, would just want to move on with like and enjoy the power. Only time would tell, but I thought there was a fair chance they wouldn't pursue me if I steered clear of London. But if I came back, brazen and bold, honour would just as surely compel the new crime boss to act. It would be madness not to go into voluntary exile.

"I doubt it," I sighed.

"Then this is goodbye?" She looked sad.

I couldn't help myself. "We'll always have Paris."

She thumped my arm and smiled.

I turned again to leave, and again she stopped me.

"The girl," Lucy said. "Is she OK?"

I shook my head. "She's not as badly hurt as she could have been, but she's going to struggle to put tonight behind her. She's harder than most of the boxers I ever faced, but they hurt her bad."

Lucy's brow furrowed. "What did they do?"

"You don't want to know."

She chewed her lower lip and kept quiet.

"If you need anything else..." she mumbled.

"Thanks, but I've plenty here. I'll try to post the gear back to you when it's over, or reimburse you if you let me know —"

"Just come through this alive," she said softly. "That'll be enough."

I smiled and hugged her. "Tell No Nose I could smell his feet," I whispered.

She stiffened, then chuckled and punched me. "You won't tell the others?"

"My lips are sealed."

"God bless, Eyrie."

"Yeah, well, we'll see," I muttered, doubtful that God was on the scene tonight.

I let myself out and hurried back to the car, thinking about Lucy and the others and how much of a wrench it would be to sever my ties with them.

I've never considered myself an expert when it comes to the human condition, or a font of all wisdom. Far from it. But there's one thing in this life that I can say with one hundred percent certainty — it's good to have friends.

Toni pulled on some of the clothes when I got back in the car, then I drove west and booked into a rundown hotel near Earl's Court. I had no notion of staying – if Smurf Mironova's people did come looking for revenge, I figured they'd check as many hotels in London as they could – but I needed a place where I could clean Toni up.

I bundled her into the bathroom as soon as we were in the room – she'd stayed in the car while I was checking in – and got her under the shower, where I washed off the blood and muck.

She stood trembling, reacting sluggishly to my commands to turn and raise her arms, and neither of us took any notice of her nudity. I rubbed the sponge over her beautiful body and never once thought of anything carnal, though I did draw the line at her lower regions and left those areas to her.

She started crying again, halfway through, and made a deep, keening sound that I had to ask her to mask, in case anyone in the neighbouring rooms heard. She did a good job of suppressing the moans after that, though she could do nothing about the tears coursing down her cheeks.

I dried her carefully, worried about the scratches and bite marks. I opened the bottle of antiseptic and treated the cuts as best I could. Her little fingers were the worst. They'd heated the blade before cutting the tips off — Toni told me this in a dead tone — so it wasn't as bad as I'd first feared, but she was in a lot of pain, even after I'd cleaned and bandaged the fingers. She should have had a doctor look at them, but we couldn't risk that. Brue could set her up with proper care when I handed her over. We only had to get through the next twelve hours. After that Brue could secure her the assistance she required and everything would be fine.

Or so I hoped.

"Feeling better?" I asked as I helped her dress again, but in clean clothes — the first, bloodstained set would have to be balled up and dumped before we left. She nodded. She was still crying. "Ready to leave?"

"We're not..." she hiccuped on a sob, "...staying?"

"No. Too easy to trace if anyone comes looking."

"So... where?"

"I know a place."

"We'll be safe?"

"I hope so."

"Then I'm ready." She wriggled her toes. "Any shoes?"

Fuck!

"Sorry. Didn't think."

"That's OK," she sniffed. "I can manage without." Drew back the curtains and stared out at the darkness. Said softly, blankly, "I've endured worse than walking around in my bare feet."

I drove east, back through the city, heading for the docks. A lot of the old, once-deserted buildings and factories had been redeveloped over the last twenty years, but there were still empty shells where a man in the know could hide. I'd come exploring here a lot as a kid, usually with friends, nothing better to do on long summer nights, moving from one temporary fortress to another, creating a world of our own. The area had changed a lot since I last swung by this way, but a few places had escaped unscathed, abandoned husks where nobody hunting us would think to look.

I drove around slowly, exploratively for a while before settling on an ancient, monstrous warehouse, once used to store exotic fruits and goods, now an exclusive home for rats, bats, cockroaches and their pals.

I parked inside – the doors were padlocked, but the wood was rotten, so I simply peeled chunks away from around the lock, and the lock came with one of them – and we climbed four flights of stairs so we'd have a good view of anybody who happened to chance by. We found sacks, cardboard, newspapers and rags, not that old, which had been used for shelter and bedding by tramps in more recent times. I picked out the least filthy scraps and made a spot for Toni to lie down. It wasn't a bed fit for a princess, but she didn't complain. I was relieved to note that she'd finally stopped crying.

"Are you hungry?" I asked.

"Not really. Thirsty."

"I should have stopped at a shop on our way." I cursed myself again. "First I forget the shoes, now this. Why didn't I think to –"

"Eyrie," she said softly, touching my arm. "Calm it. You've done good tonight. Don't beat yourself up because of a few minor details, OK?"

I smiled gratefully and placed my hand over hers, squeezing it gently, being careful not to hurt the amputated finger. "OK."

I only meant to sit by her side, but she wanted me to lie down and hold her. So I did. Took her in my arms and felt her thin body shivering and convulsing, partly from the cold, mostly from her ordeal. She whimpered and wept, even when she dropped off to sleep. I held her close and tried soothing her with kind words and soft crooning.

Sometimes she'd start thrashing, and wake screaming and cursing, beating my chest. I held her tighter on those occasions, rubbed her head and back, let her bite my shoulder if she needed. I could take the pain. Compared with what she'd been through, it was nothing.

In moments of calm, she'd cry quietly and tell me what had happened to her, describing the people who'd assaulted her, the women who'd laughed while they cut her, the men who'd grimaced ghoulishly while they masturbated over her, a giggling Smurf Mironova coordinating it all like some warped conductor. She vowed to remember everyone who had tortured and humiliated her, so that she could track them down later and make them pay.

"Every fucking one of them," she reiterated harshly, looking her normal self as she growled it. "I won't forget. I won't forgive. I'll get even with them all, I don't care how long it takes."

I listened without replying. I knew a thing or two about waiting to get even, but wasn't sure whether or not to bring up my past. I felt it might help us bond, and provide her with some measure of comfort by proving to her that it was possible to get through something as dreadful as this. But at the same time this was all about her, and I was reluctant to talk about my own pain, for fear she might think I was trying to top her suffering, that I was turning this into one of those, "You think *that's* bad? Wait until you hear what happened to *me*!" conversations.

I didn't want to listen to the finer details of how they'd hurt her, but she had to get it out, had to speak while the wounds were fresh. This was her way of dealing with the pain and overcoming it, confronting the cruel reality of her situation head-on, so that it could have no hold over her later.

So I let her talk, and at times I wept with her, and I thought about Zahra and Dancing James, and wondered how we'd come to live in such a debased world, and I was sorry I'd never believed in God because at least then I'd have had something bigger to blame, some high overseer to hold accountable.

"They cut off my fingers!" she screamed at one point, and began thrusting her hands at me. Tried ripping off the bandages to show me. I told her I'd seen them, but she wouldn't stop, couldn't stop. Hysteria was setting in and I wasn't sure how to help dispel it. So, even though I'd been hesitant to talk about myself and how the world had turned against me in the desert, I started to tell her, hoping it would distract and console her, and prevent her from doing any more damage to herself.

"I knew another woman who was tortured like you," I said softly. "They cut off her fingers too, five of them, all the digits on her left hand."

Toni stopped tugging at the bandages and stared at me.

"Her name was Zahra," I continued, holding Toni, remembering the times I'd held Zahra when she was alive, and the last time, when she was limp, ruined, still. "I was in the Army, serving in the desert."

"What desert?" Toni asked.

I shook my head. "It doesn't matter. They're all the same. Listen. Zahra was a local woman. We were encouraged by our superiors to mingle with the locals, get them on our side, convince them we were there fighting for them, for their future. But we were never supposed to fall in love with them…"

I hadn't meant for it to happen. Hadn't thought it could. There was such a divide between us and them, our culture and theirs. The men kept the women away from us to the best of their abilities, wary of us, hostile.

Zahra was in a different situation to many of her countrywomen. As a nurse, she had more freedom of movement than most, but aside from that her father was a moderate and had always granted her plenty of leeway. He had lived for a time in England as a young man. He'd have happily stayed and raised his family there, but he loved his home country, hated to see it suffering, and believed it was his duty to return and do what he could to help defy the small-minded, power-hoarding tyrants, and restore law and order.

At first it was innocent. I met Zahra a few times by chance and we chatted. She was always looking to practise her English. I'd tell her about London, what it was like, my experiences growing up there. She'd tell me about the desert, the troubles she'd faced all her life, the things a woman needed to do in order to survive in a society like hers.

Things progressed by themselves before we could anticipate and sidestep them, as they sometimes do, and without our quite knowing how, the friendship became something much, much more.

"Was she beautiful?" Toni asked, lying almost motionless in my arms, the calmest she'd been since I rescued her.

"No," I said. "A good-looking woman, but not the sort who'd turn heads. It wasn't about physical attraction. I mean, there was plenty of that too, but I wasn't looking for an exotic fling. I knew the danger she could find herself in if she got involved with an outsider like me. I wouldn't have put her in that position if I'd had a choice. If it had just been about sex, I'd have gone to one of the brothels over there."

"They have brothels in places like that?" Toni was surprised.

I smiled bitterly. "They have brothels everywhere."

We didn't make love many times. There were few opportunities and it wasn't that big a deal for either of us, as we thought we would have plenty of time for lovemaking in the years to come.

I'd made up my mind, when it became clear to me that we'd both fallen in love, to convert. I'd never been religious and could happily pay lip service to any god. I'd serve out my contract, return when I was a free man, accept her beliefs, marry her, spend the rest of my life with her. I didn't care that she lived in a hellhole. I'd have settled anywhere just to be with her.

"I can see where this is going," Toni murmured. "Her people found out and butchered her."

"No," I sighed. "It wasn't that simple. In a way I wish it was."

Jim *Dancing* James was one of my fellow soldiers. We'd never got along. There are some people in this world who just rub you up the wrong way, and James was one of those. We'd prickled at one another when we first met, and our mutual dislike had grown into full enmity over the months and years. Being totally honest, it wasn't a one-way street. This wasn't a bad guy/good guy situation, at least not for a long time. I gave as spitefully as I got, and did as much as he did to fan the flames of animosity between us.

Every verbal exchange involved one of us sneering at the other. We'd had a few proper fights, but there'd been no clear winner — he'd been a boxer too, an equal match for me, and his nickname dated back to the way he used to dance round the ring. We'd probably have continued in that petty, largely harmless fashion until our superiors noticed and shipped one of us off to another unit, but then James took the unwarranted and shocking decision to escalate hostilities.

"I did my best to keep my relationship with Zahra secret," I told Toni. "I knew I'd be moved if word leaked."

But Dancing James found out. Something aroused his suspicions – maybe I'd stopped reacting to his jibes, making him wonder why I was smiling all the time instead of scowling – and he started shadowing me. I was blissfully unaware of the surveillance and carried on as normal. He saw me meet with Zahra and trailed us around. He noted our secret meeting places, the rooms in isolated areas where we would get together whenever we could.

He hatched a plan to destroy me.

"We were on patrol," I said, tears rolling down my cheeks, crying as freely as Toni had earlier. I hadn't told anyone this story in its entirety. I'd been carrying it with me since the desert, like Christ lugging his cross, and assumed I'd carry it unvoiced for the rest of my life. "Someone had given us a tip-off, sent us to a building outside the city where we were based. It was one of the buildings where Zahra and I used to meet."

I didn't know it was her at first. There was a woman's corpse strapped to a chair in the middle of the room, but it could have been any woman. Much of her face had been burnt and carved open. All the fingers of her left hand had been amputated. Her clothes had been removed and her breasts had been amputated too. Even though this was a familiar building, I didn't think (didn't *want* to think) that the woman in the chair might be my lover. We hadn't been scheduled to meet. No reason why it should be her remains and not some other woman's.

Then Dancing James leant over and whispered in my ear, "Look familiar?"

And straightaway I saw it all. It was Zahra. James had found out and tortured and killed her. He'd made it look like the work of her own people, but I could tell from his smirk that it had been him.

Toni's eyes were round but she didn't say anything. Another person would have been shocked, would have asked how anyone could be that vile, how a man could kill an innocent woman just to hurt a guy he didn't like. But Toni moved in circles where this wouldn't come as a surprise. She'd seen the underbelly of the world and knew what certain sick people were like, how they sometimes killed for no good reason, just because they wanted to draw a reaction, just because they could.

In that building in the desert, I broke ranks and threw myself at Zahra, clutched her tight, howled like a madman, tried to scream life back into her shattered, wretched form. The other members of my unit hung back, stunned, not sure what was going on.

Distraught, I drew my gun and turned to target Dancing James, to kill him as he had killed the love of my life. But he'd anticipated that and was ready for me. Clubbed me senseless. Handcuffed me. Laughed as I was led away, leaving Zahra behind for a stranger to untie and examine and dispose of.

I fell silent. Toni gave me a hug and I smiled at her through my tears.

"Did you report him?" she asked.

"No," I sobbed. "There was no point. I couldn't prove anything."

"Did you kill him?" she pressed.

I stopped crying. Started wiping the tears away. Stared over her head and said nothing until I was back in control of myself.

"I was released early from my contract," I said. "My commanding officers weren't stupid. They realised I'd had an affair with the dead woman, though they didn't know about James' role in her torment and execution. They thought she'd been killed by her own lot and I didn't try to convince them otherwise. They felt sorry for me, and when they saw that I couldn't continue, they made it easy for me to bail."

I wiped away the last of the tears and smiled weakly at Toni. "What you went through tonight... it's awful, something you'll never be able to forget. But as hard as this might be to accept right now, it could have been a lot worse." I stroked her face tenderly. "They didn't rape you. And you're alive."

"You think that's a good thing?" she sniffed.

"Yes," I said.

"Maybe I'd be better off dead," she croaked.

I shook my head. "You're strong, like Zahra was strong. You'll find a way to live with this, the way she would have, no matter what James did to her. Only she was never given that chance."

Toni stared at me, tears welling up in her eyes again.

"I wish someone loved me the way you loved her," she moaned.

I touched her nose playfully.

"Don't be so sure that maybe they won't, one day," I said gently.

She trembled when I said that, and clung to me, and started sobbing again, but this time not quite as desperately as before.

"Can I confess something?" she asked.

The sun was now high in the sky – another scorcher of a day – but it was cool in the shade of the damp old building. I'd gone for a walk earlier, found a shop, bought a few bottles of water and something to eat. I had to hold the plastic cups for her when she was drinking, as her hands were too sore to grip.

"Fire away," I said.

"I thought you were one of them."

I frowned. "What do you mean?"

"When they came to the apartment and took me. I thought you'd left me for them, that you were in league with Smurf Mironova. I hated you more than any of the others. Even when they were beating me and cutting me, you were the one I wanted to kill the most. I thought you'd betrayed me."

I stared at her solemnly. "And when I showed up?"

Her head hung low. "I thought you'd come to take your turn when they started," she whispered.

"No," I said softly. "I would never..."

"I know that now," she cried, "but in the room, when I saw you coming through the door and thought that was a sign that the torment was about to kick up a level, I almost abandoned the fight. That was nearly the final nail in this coffin."

She tapped the side of her head and turned to look at me directly.

"I'd suffered monstrously, and assumed worse was to come. It would have been easy to go crazy, to retreat into full-blown madness and lose myself. But I clung in there, memorising the faces of my abusers, telling myself I'd escape and come back to kill them all. I purposely held on to my mind and my humanity. I knew it would haunt me forever but I was determined not to let them break me. I didn't want to give the bastards the satisfaction of seeing me crack. No matter what they did to me, they couldn't truly get to me. They didn't hurt me *here*."

She touched her left breast, her heart.

"But when I saw you..." she went on. "When you came in,

and I saw your face rising like a sorry-looking moon behind that fucker's arse, and I thought you were there to rape me, to laugh, to watch and help record it... I nearly crumbled. I came that close–" she held her fingers millimetres apart, "–to losing my mind, my heart, my hope." She smiled wanly. "My soul, if it isn't already a blackened, shrivelled kernel of a thing after all that I've done in my life."

She touched my hand, maintaining eye contact. "You mattered to me, Eyrie Brown. The rest were beasts but you were human. I hated you with everything I had in that moment, but you mattered. Understand?"

I could only stare, nod wordlessly and caress her battered hand.

When the pain got very bad, I remembered her love of movies and turned talk to Tony Curtis and *Some Like It Hot*. Hard drugs were what she really needed, but we had to make do with what we had.

"Remember when he met Marilyn on the beach?" I asked as she shivered and sweated, her hands balled into pitiful fists. "He put on a terrible English accent, pretended to be the owner of Shell, and she believed him, and –"

"Cary... Grant," Toni gasped.

"What?"

"He was... pretending to be Cary Grant. Acting like him, aping the way... he spoke. Taking the... piss."

"Really?"

"Yeah."

"I didn't know that." I chuckled. "Sly old Tony."

She grimaced as another wave of pain hit. I hurried into the next anecdote and we talked about the shaking of the maracas. I was able to tell her that had been the director Billy Wilder's idea, to allow the audience time to laugh before the next line, and I told her a bit more about him, because she only knew about the stars, had never taken much of an interest in directors or writers.

We tried thinking of the old actor's name, the guy with the killer line at the end of the movie – "*Nobody's perfect*" – but drew a blank. Couldn't even name another film that he'd been in. We also couldn't think of any other movie where such a great final line had been given to a peripheral character.

It was meaningless chatter but it helped distract her. She was in pain, in shock. Her pupils would dilate every so often and she'd stiffen. Her fingers would twitch as if she was being pumped full of electricity. She was handling it better than most people would have, but you don't get over something like what she'd been through in a hurry, no matter how tough you are.

"Did you know Tony Curtis invented rap?" I asked when she started to shake again.

"What?" she gawped.

"That's what he believed anyway. I read it in an interview. See…"

And it diverted her attention. And I told another story after that. And another. And kept on going, as long as I had to, as long as it helped.

I moved the plastic cup away from her lips. I was making sure she drank a lot of water. We used one of the corners in the next room as a toilet. I'd carried her there the first few times, but she was starting to get some strength back and was able to make the trip by herself in the afternoon.

She licked a couple of stray drops of water from her lips. Her eyes met mine and she smiled. "You would have made a good nurse."

"Maybe I'll retrain."

She laughed softly, then the smile faded. Her gaze stayed locked on mine.

I could feel my heart picking up speed. It would have been simple and natural. Just a kiss, nothing else. Almost as innocent and meaningless as the peck on the cheek I'd given to Lucy before I departed.

I felt my head angling towards hers, my lips opening as hers were opening.

I stopped.

Sat back.

Shook my head.

"No, Toni."

"No?"

She looked down at her ravaged body, thinking at first that I was rejecting her because of her wounds and humiliation. Then it clicked and she gave a little sigh.

"Because of Lewis?" she pouted.

"Because of Lewis," I confirmed.

"He doesn't matter. After what we've been through, what you did for me..."

"I only did my job."

I hated the words even before they'd left my mouth, but they had to be said. She was a gangster's moll, as they would have phrased it in an old movie like *Some Like It Hot*. Wouldn't be much point in my saving her if I let something dumb like this happen. We'd both be up to our necks in it then, in an even worse situation than we were right now.

"I was paid to look after you. And I did. And that's all there is between us. All there ever can be."

She nodded wearily. "I guess you're right," she said softly. "I'm pretty confused at the moment. I suppose I'd feel close to anyone who'd done me such a good turn. I misread the look in your eyes, seeing what I wanted to see."

"Yeah," I agreed, feeling my heart burn in my chest, knowing she knew she'd misread nothing. I wanted her. As the old saying goes, to have and to hold. But she couldn't be mine any more than Zahra could be, and I'd just have to learn to live with her absence, as I'd learnt to live with the absence of that other great love of my life. Hell, it was way too early to even assume that Toni would or could have been a great love, so I'd miss her a lot less than I missed Zahra.

Or so I told myself.

So I tried to believe.

Toni was silent a while. Then she said, "You think we'll ever meet again?"

"No," I said.

"You ever *want* to meet again?"

I didn't answer for a long beat. Then, "Here," I said. "Have another drink."

"I just had one."

I held the rim of the cup to her cracked lips.

"I know."

And she could tell I wanted her to stop speaking, because this conversation was tearing me apart inside. So she drank, and we lay there saying nothing, but I was all too painfully aware that more was being said in that silence than we perhaps could ever have said with words.

Later, she rose and stretched. Staggered, then found her footing. Took a couple of deep breaths and bent over. Touched her toes. Stood. Went through the routine a few more times. Swung her arms from left to right, wincing, teeth gritted, but forcing her body to obey her command. Taking back control.

"Better?" I asked.

She grunted. "They gave me some going over, but I don't think anything's damaged inside."

"You'll need a doctor to determine that."

She shrugged. "Maybe."

"You think you'll be able to make the meet?" I asked.

"Sure."

"Will Brue understand when I explain what happened?"

She nodded. "He's probably already heard. If not, or if he's only been told part of the story, we'll fill him in. When I tell him what you risked, how you saved me, he'll appreciate the guts it took. He won't blame you for what they did to me. It wasn't your fault."

"If I hadn't left you tied up…" I muttered.

She scowled. "Well, yeah, obviously *that* was your fault." She laughed. "But we all make mistakes. Like I said earlier, I won't ever forgive those bastards for what they did – and I *will* make them pay – but you… yeah, you, I forgive."

I smiled at her but inside I was cold, because I couldn't forgive myself. I should never have left her. Brue was at fault too, for telling me to come to his place and leave her where she was. But I was her bodyguard. I'd been paid to protect her. I should have taken all possible precautions, regardless of what my employer told me. It would be easy to pass the blame, but I wouldn't give myself that get-out. I'd let her down and that would eat away at me forever.

Then again, if I'd stayed, I might have been taken by surprise by Smurf and his men, caught with my back to the wall. I could have ended up with her in the room in that building behind the casino, both of us on the receiving end of a chain of indiscriminate rapists. And there'd have been no rescue then, for either of us.

"When do we leave?" she asked.

I checked my watches. "Another couple of hours."

"That long?" She sighed. Then, after stealing a look in my direction, she added with a wry, sad little smile, "That soon?"

We talked about our lives, our childhoods, growing up, old lovers. She already knew about Zahra, but I told her about the other ladies there'd been, none as important to me as Zahra, but each meaningful in some way.

Toni's life was more convoluted than mine. There wasn't time to cover more than a fraction of it, but she filled me in on the main points. She'd had to mature fast or go under. Her father a small-time crook on the English side of the Scottish Borders. He'd never paid much attention to her, in and out of prison as she was growing up. Her mother not much more of a homemaker, revelling in open affairs, sometimes going off for weeks or months at a time with the men she fell for. Went one night when Toni was eleven and never came back. Toni searched for her later in life but never did find out if she ran away to establish a new life with a lover or met with a messy end.

She grew into a wild teenager who caused trouble wherever she went. Heading for the same sort of downward spiral as her father. Then she met a guy who trained her how to focus her rage and energy. He'd been a surrogate father, an instructor, eventually a lover. Taught her how to fight, how to live, how to kill.

He introduced her to Brue when she was seventeen. She did some jobs for the London-based gangster. An impressed Brue called her his child assassin. He made a few passes at her but she was true to her mentor and Brue respected that, never overstepped the mark.

Her saviour died in a car accident when she was days shy of her nineteenth birthday. A hit and run victim. Impossible to tell if it had been an accident or if it had been arranged by one of his enemies — people like them always had enemies who were keen to settle old scores, and question marks had to be employed every time one of them fell prey to an "accident."

Brue proved to be a rock for her while she was grieving, and they'd grown closer over the following months, though they never did become lovers. She moved to London to work for him. Great times for a while, but she was forced to flee the city after some nasty encounters with Jeb Howard. She set up as an independent operator and her and Brue stayed in touch. He passed scraps of work her way every now and then, if they didn't involve her having to travel to London, and their paths had crossed occasionally over the years, in cities like Cardiff, Glasgow, Paris, Berlin.

He'd called her last week to ask if she'd return to London for a few days, said he had a guy lined up to protect her while she was here, but advised her to lay low while she was in town.

"Good advice," I couldn't help interjecting.

She glowered at me. "Laying low's for cowards."

"You say that even now, after all that's happened?" I asked.

She nodded, then had the good grace to grimace. "Well, in retrospect, maybe I'd have laid a *bit* lower," she said grudgingly, and managed a small laugh at her own expense, which was a positive sign.

She wasn't sure what Brue had called her back for, but guessed he had a special job laid on that he didn't trust to his regular team. She'd harboured hopes that he was going to sic her on Howard. As I'd already seen, she was a girl who knew how to hold a grudge.

My life was tame in comparison with hers, but she listened intently. Wanted to know what I'd done before the Army, why I'd entered the Forces, what boxing had been like. I found myself opening up like I hadn't since with Zahra, telling her of my dreams, my fears, the loneliness, the drinking.

I even came close to telling her about Dancing James and what had happened after I'd been discharged, the photos I'd hung beside my bed and then taken down, how similar I was to her in certain ways. But the afternoon got away from us. In the middle of deciding whether or not I dared open up to her completely, I checked one watch, then the other, and saw that the time for talking had passed.

It was time to get ready and leave.

"Have everything?" I asked.

"Uh-huh," she grunted, easing on a pair of slippers that I'd bought when I went shopping earlier.

"Bandages OK?" I'd changed them recently.

"Fine."

I took a deep breath. "Nothing left to stay for then, is there?"

"No," she sighed. "Guess not." She looked around glumly, as regretful as I was that this quiet time of sharing and reflection was over.

Then she spat purposefully and started for the stairs.

In the car, driving across London to our meeting with Lewis Brue.

I kept my gaze on the road.

Toni looked inwards.

I didn't speak to her during the journey, or even glance at her. Didn't dare, for fear it might lead to me hitting the brakes and succumbing to the suicidal madness of unleashed passion.

THIRTEEN — TWISTS

We were due to meet with Lewis Brue in the bookies where he had first made me his offer. The street outside was almost deserted, a quiet Sunday evening, the city in slumber mode. I pulled up in front of the entrance, checked to make sure nobody was loitering nearby, and we got out of the car.

Toni was able to walk by herself but I let her lean on me all the same. Probably the last chance I'd ever get to hold her. Be a shame to waste it.

Rabbit opened the door and nodded respectfully to Toni. He'd obviously been filled in since our last meeting, as he wasn't surprised to see her.

"You're to go up," Rabbit told me, then turned politely to Toni. "Not you, Miss Curtis. You're to come with me. Mr Brue said he'll meet us in a while to explain what this is all about."

"All right." She let go of me, coughed, then smiled. "So long, Eyrie Brown."

"So long, Toni Curtis. I'd shake hands, but..."

"Hah," she said flatly, then winked and let Rabbit lead her away. I watched until the door closed, then headed upstairs with a heavy sigh.

Lewis Brue was by the window, looking out, no doubt checking on Toni and Rabbit.

"I heard about last night," he said without turning, and it was impossible to tell from his tone if he was pissed or pleased. "Is she OK?"

"She'll live," I said.

"Can you be more specific?"

"Lots of people hit her, bit her, sliced her. They cut off the tips of her two little fingers. They were going to gang rape her, but I got there before they started."

"A terrible affair," he murmured, then turned to look at me. "What sort of shape is she in, physically and mentally, in your opinion?"

I shrugged. "I think not too bad physically, although a doctor will need to check to be sure. Mentally..." I hesitated. "She's hurting in all sorts of ways, but they haven't destroyed her. She seems to be coping, but there's been a lot of tears, and I'm sure there are more to come. It will be difficult but I'm confident she'll get through this intact."

"A psychiatrist as well as a bodyguard and taxi driver." He smiled. "A man of many talents."

"I was just –" I started to defend myself, but he waved a hand to silence me.

"Relax, I was busting your balls, as our American cousins would put it. You've been through quite a bit this weekend, if the buzzing on the grapevine's to be believed. You really attacked Smurf Mironova's joint by yourself, killed him and several of his associates to get her back?"

"Toni killed them," I said. "I just got her out of there."

"*Just*." He shook his head admiringly. "I knew I'd picked a good man but I'd no idea you were this resourceful. You should have demanded more money. A man of your abilities can name his price."

"I'm happy with what you paid me."

"I haven't heard that too many times in my life," he chortled. Then his smile faded. "I'm curious. Why didn't you tell Rabbit when you discovered she'd been taken? You were out of the game. Why deal yourself back in?"

"I wasn't sure how you'd take it," I admitted. "Thought you might blame me for her disappearance, or maybe think I'd arranged it, that I'd cut a separate deal with Mironova and was conning you."

"I'm not that paranoid," he said.

"I'm sure you're not, but I didn't fancy chancing it. Anyway, you'd said you couldn't get involved if others found out that she was in London and made a move on her, so I didn't think you'd try to rescue her."

"And you didn't want to abandon her, leave her in the hands of her captors?"

I nodded.

"You're an odd one, Eyrie Brown. Can I get you a drink?"

"I wouldn't say no."

Lewis Brue laughed and fetched a couple of bottles of beer. I could have done with something stronger but it was a good beginning. I'd hit the hard stuff later, when I was somewhere far from London. Go on the bender of all benders, try to forget the blood, the bodies, the fact that I'd never see Toni again.

"It's over, isn't it?" I asked.

"Absolutely," he said.

"What about the police? Smurf Mironova's men?"

Brue sniffed. "The latter won't be a problem. Smurf wasn't liked. His guys backed him because he made money for them, not because they were loyal. None of them will care about settling scores with you. They'll be too busy fighting among themselves to replace him.

"As for the police... If word seeps back to them, as it may, given all the corpses and witnesses, they might drag you in for questioning, but they won't have any firm evidence relating either to the quarrel in DEL'S or the riot at the casino. Any CCTV footage has already been wiped, and in the unlikely event that someone grasses, one of my team will politely persuade them to retract their statement. You'll be fine."

I sipped my beer, surprised but relieved. "So I don't have to leave London?"

He shook his head. "In fact it would be better if you didn't bail for the next few days, in case the police do come looking for you. An innocent man doesn't have to run and hide, right?"

By the sound of things, I'd be able to hit the rum in my own apartment once the dust had settled. That would make life a lot easier – I hadn't been looking forward to relocating – although I'd bid a dramatic farewell to Lucy, so I could expect a fair amount of ribbing from the gang when I returned to my job.

"How did you hear about my run-in with Smurf?" I asked.

Brue snorted. "The whole city's heard by now. Not the sort of thing you can keep quiet very long."

I stared at the bottle, mulling over everything that had happened, feeling uneasy about something. "News spreads quickly through your circle, doesn't it?" I said, thinking out loud.

"Oh yes," he beamed. "We do love to gossip."

"Then wasn't it a mistake to leave Toni tied up in my apartment, unprotected?"

He frowned. "It was a risk, sure, but as I told you at the time, I didn't want to involve any of my men."

"But you've involved Rabbit now," I noted.

"Now's different," Brue said. "It was always my plan to bring Rabbit in on this if we made it to this point."

"I see," I muttered, lying through my back teeth, not seeing at all.

"You think I'm holding something back?" Brue asked.

"It seems odd," I said hesitantly, wary of angering him, but needing to scratch the itch that was building inside me now that I was free at last to relax and think. "You could have posted a guy outside my apartment, not told him who was inside, just to intervene if anyone turned up who looked like they shouldn't be there."

Brue shrugged. "I thought she'd be safe. There was no reason to suspect that anyone would target you so swiftly. Toni has lots of enemies, but the only one actively seeking her was Jeb Howard, and we had nothing to fear from him. I knew that Smurf would be pissed about his sister, and figured there was a chance he'd come looking for you, but I didn't expect him to pull his shit together as quickly as he did. Him turning up that night at your place was as much a shock for me as it was for you."

"Still..." I mumbled, unable to let it lie.

"Eyrie." He held up his hands in a steadying gesture. "There's nothing certain in my world. We run all sorts of wild risks and do our best to deal with the consequences when things flip against us. In retrospect I should have told you to bring Toni with you, but I gambled that she'd be safe. It was a mistake, but it's the sort of minor misjudgement men like me make all the time. Anyway, I got the most important call right — I put her in *your* hands. You were my insurance card and you more than justified my faith in you."

I smiled at the flattery and took a swig of the beer. I was feeling embarrassed. Lewis Brue had treated me decently at every turn. It was petty of me to point out his errors to him.

"Sorry," I mumbled. "I spoke out of turn."

"No need to apologise," he grinned. "I remember the night we met, when I'd suffered the sort of barrage that you've endured this weekend. I probably said a few things I shouldn't have too. No hard feelings. Let me get you another beer."

He slapped my back as he passed. I smiled wearily, finished off the last of my bottle and waited for him to return.

As I was waiting, my embarrassment turned to suspicion again. I wanted to let the whole thing lie and get out of there, not even bother with the second bottle of beer. But one of Brue's comments had set alarm bells ringing. I told myself I was being irrational, but I couldn't ignore it. The memory of Toni lying on the bed in that building, naked and abused, wouldn't let me.

As a whistling Lewis Brue re-entered the room, a beer in either hand, I said, "Jeb Howard."

Brue stopped in the doorway and squinted at me. "What about him?"

"Just now you said we had nothing to fear from him, but previously I got the impression he was the main threat, the reason you had to tread so carefully, why you hired me and not one of your own men."

"This is true," Brue said cautiously, "but you told me Golding Mironova couldn't have made contact with him, so there was no reason to think he might target you."

"But Smurf found out about me," I pushed, "and you keep telling me he wasn't the most clued-in."

"He found out about *you*," Brue said. "Not Toni. That was just a lucky break for him — or not so lucky, as things worked out. I'm sure Jeb Howard heard about the shooting in DEL'S, but he had no interest in Golding Mironova, so he would have had no interest in the guy and his gal who killed her."

"Even so," I said stubbornly, "there was a chance that someone else in the pub might have recognised Toni. I can't understand why you told me to leave her in my apartment. It wasn't an oversight. It was a truly dumb move. And I don't think you're the sort of guy who makes too many truly dumb moves."

Brue stood there silently, staring at me, clinking the bottles together.

Then he sighed.

"You've got a whiff of something, haven't you?" he said. "Won't stop till you get to the bottom of it all, even if it drags you down to a place where you don't want to go, where you know you *shouldn't* go. Am I right?"

"I need to know," I said quietly. "I never wanted to know more than was good for me. I asked as few questions as possible. But when you tell me one thing, then say the opposite, that makes me curious, and I reckon I've earned the right to an answer or two."

Brue tilted his head. "Again, this is true, and I don't begrudge you the answers, but you might not like what you hear."

"I'm sure I won't," I said miserably. "But I'm asking all the same."

Brue studied me seriously, still clinking the bottles together.

"You spent a lot of time with Toni this weekend," he said.

"Yeah."

"Did you fuck her?"

"No," I said tightly.

"Easy."

He sat down and passed me a beer. I took it reluctantly and put it down on the floor, keeping my hands free.

"I just want to know where you and her stand," Brue said softly.

"We don't stand anywhere," I told him. "You paid me to look after her — I did. You told me it could be dangerous — it was. You said bring her here — I brought her. I've played it straight all the way down the line."

"So there's nothing between the two of you?"

"No."

"Good. Then you can deal with it."

"Deal with what?" I frowned.

"The truth." He took a long draught of beer, then said, "I'm giving her to Jeb Howard. That's why I brought her back to London. I'm patching up our differences and Toni's a peace offering."

I stared at Lewis Brue, ashen-faced. "Will Howard…?"

"…kill her?" He sniffed and tried to pretend it didn't matter to him. "Yes. He's hated her for a long time, but Toni murdered one of his best friends a while back, and that pushed the matter into a whole different arena. He's offering big money for her head — not that I'm doing it for that. I'm tossing her to him for free, to stop us going to war over a load of other shit that's been bubbling up between us these last several months. It's a war I don't want, a war I can't afford, and most crucially, it's a war I wouldn't win. I'm very fond of Toni, in a fatherly way, but it's her or everything I've built over the years, so…" He shrugged uncomfortably.

My head was spinning. I endured all that… rescued her… held her in my arms as she trembled… didn't even kiss her… restrained myself because it was the right thing to do… and now…

"Rabbit's taking her to Jeb Howard?" I asked in a choked voice.

"Yeah."

"Where?"

"I can't tell you that."

Instinct kicked in before I could consider my actions. I pulled my Hi-Power and let him stare down the barrel of the weapon he'd supplied me with.

"I don't want to use this," I said. "Just tell me where he's taking her."

Brue gazed at the gun without any apparent fear, then glared at me.

"You *did* fuck her," he snarled.

"No. I didn't. Where's Rabbit taking her?"

"You can't save her, Brown. She's too hot. If someone like me can't keep her from the wolves, how the fuck will a nobody like you?"

"Let me worry about that. Tell me where she is or I'll put a bullet through your knee." The same threat I'd used with Craig Haine, but I didn't see any need to be overly creative on that front.

Brue paused, trying to judge if I was serious or not, if he could talk me round or if I'd make good on my threat. Must have seen from the look in my eyes that this wasn't the time to gamble.

"Behind Beckton Gas Works," he growled. "Just past City Airport. There's a patch of wasteland. Howard will be parked up, waiting."

"How many with him?"

"Not many, I'd imagine. He knows he's safe, nothing to fear from me, no reason for me to cross him."

"Will he kill her there?"

"He hasn't shared his plans with me," Brue said, "but Jeb Howard isn't known for his patience, and unlike our deceased friend, Smurf Mironova, he's not into torture. When there's business to attend to, he cracks on and attends to it. I'd say there's a very good chance he'll deal with Toni as soon as Rabbit hands her over."

I started backing towards the door, never lowering my aim.

"You won't catch them," he said. "They've too big a lead on you."

"I'm a cabbie," I reminded him. "I know this city better than Rabbit. I should be able to make up ground on them."

I reached the doorway. About to slip out when I stopped.

Brue laughed cruelly. "It's just struck you," he said as if this was all a joke to him. "Rabbit has a mobile. The second you step out, I'll phone him and we'll re-schedule with Howard. You'll be chasing ghosts."

I stared at Brue wordlessly.

"Now you're considering your options," he went on, still in that jocular tone. "You could kill me, but you're not a killer, and I've been good to you, paid you as I promised. That wouldn't mean much to a lot of guys, but a man like you respects a respectful man like me. You won't execute me in cold blood when I've done nothing to you to merit it."

I looked around the office.

"You could tie me up," Brue said, and his reading of my intentions was starting to irritate me, "but you've no idea what my itinerary for the rest of the day might be like, if some of my guys are due to drop by and pick me up. If I'm freed before you make it to the rendezvous, I'll ring Rabbit and it's game up.

"Let this go," he said as kindly as he could. "She was dead the minute she returned to London. Hell, she was dead the minute she took up a gun as a kid and found it a comfortable fit. You can't save the damned, Eyrie Brown."

I went on staring at him. He was right. I couldn't kill him, and leaving him tied up here was too much of a risk. That left...

I hurried to the desk, mindful of the passing seconds, and rooted through the drawers. Found a roll of masking tape.

"Hands behind your back," I ordered.

His smile slipped. This wasn't what he had expected.

"You're fucking joking, aren't you?" he snapped.

"You're coming with me. Hands."

"Brown, think about what you're doing. I like you. I brought you in on this to reward you. Don't make an enemy of me now."

"Your hands," I barked.

Lewis Brue tapped his chin with two heavy fingers, then turned and crossed his hands behind his back. I frisked him, took his gun away, then wound the tape tightly round his wrists.

"This is the wrong play," he said politely but angrily.

"Maybe," I conceded, "but it's the only play I can make."

We marched down the stairs, out the front door and into Mickey Goodnews' car, Brue in the passenger seat beside me. I started the engine and looked sideways at him. "I don't want a long discussion. If you start yapping, I'll tape your mouth shut and stick you in the boot. Are we clear?"

"You're the boss," he said with a sneer.

I put my foot down and aimed for the East, and we sped through the city like the devil himself was hot on our scorching tail.

I took every shortcut I could imagine, and went against traffic on a few one way streets, figuring they'd be largely free of cars this late on a Sunday. I made it across the city faster than I ever had before, and as we closed on our destination I spotted a car ahead of us, turning off to the left.

"Is that them?" I asked, slowing down.

Brue squinted. "Perhaps. They're too far ahead to be sure."

"But that's where Jeb Howard is supposed to be waiting, right?"

"I think so," he said sourly.

Good enough for me. I zipped along until I came to the place where the car had turned. There was a footpath, then a wire fence that ran all the way along this stretch, trees and bushes growing behind it. A section of the fence had been pinned back to create an opening, and I could see tyre tracks advancing through the bushes, which grew thinly here.

I pushed through slowly, the bushes parting around the car. There was a large area of barren land just beyond, more trees and bushes on the far side, an old road cutting through them. I could see Rabbit's car just disappearing from sight down the road. He was going at a crawl, so I crawled too.

I checked the gun while I was covering the last short stretch. I hadn't thought to reload after the Smurf incident, so I ejected the magazine and replaced it with a fresh clip.

"That thing was empty?" Brue barked.

"Maybe, maybe not," I smiled. "But it sure isn't empty now."

"Fuck!" He thrust forward in his seat, as though to headbutt the window, but stopped short and sat back. "You're some chancer, Brown," he said with grudging respect. "I'm liking you more and more. What say we turn round and forget this? You were under a lot of pressure. You weren't thinking straight. I can forgive."

"I told you I didn't want to hear you talking," I growled.

"We're practically there now. What harm can a few words do?"

"None to me. Plenty to you. Shut it. I'm trying to concentrate."

There was a large quadrangle beyond the trees, surrounded by shrubbery on all sides. A limo was parked in the middle. Four men were standing by it, one slightly ahead of the other three.

Rabbit had parked close to the limo. He and Toni were out and walking. Her hands were behind her back and her head was hanging low. Rabbit glanced over his shoulder when he heard my car but Toni's head never moved.

I stopped behind Rabbit's car and got out. The four men by the limo were staring at me curiously. They could see the fuming Lewis Brue and were no doubt wondering what he was doing here. The middle-aged guy in front – Jeb Howard, I assumed – turned to address his men. None of them looked overly alarmed. They weren't expecting an ambush.

I drew the Hi-Power and fired. Aimed low, for their legs. Didn't want to kill unless I had to.

I hit one of the guards and he went down screaming. The others cursed, pulled their weapons and shot at me. Bullets ripped into the concrete floor around me and a couple whizzed by my ears. I was exposed, one against three, terrible odds, but there was nothing I could do except keep firing and advancing, and pray that I got lucky.

I winged another guard and dared to start hoping. But then a bullet struck my right forearm and the Hi-Power flew from my hand as it was snapped backwards.

The men smiled mercilessly, held fire and shifted their feet to take more careful aim. I knew I was finished and prepared myself to die.

Before I could make my peace with any gods who might have tuned in for the show, Jeb Howard's chest exploded in a burst of red and he slumped without even a scream. The guards flinched and stared, shocked, no idea what was happening. I didn't know either, but when I switched my focus from Jeb Howard and his men to Toni and Rabbit, it all became clear.

Rabbit was standing tall, a gun in hand.

And so was Toni.

It had been a ruse. Her hands had been free the whole time. This *was* a trap, but not the one Jeb Howard had been expecting. Toni wasn't being delivered. She had been sent to *make* a delivery.

Jeb Howard's guards fell fast, ripped apart by a shower of bullets. I scrabbled for my gun and picked it up with my left hand, in case my assistance was required, but I needn't have bothered. Their hesitation had robbed them of any chance they might have stood, and they never even got to return fire. They died like spasming puppets, along with the one that I'd downed, falling in a lifeless heap next to their slain master.

Toni pranced ahead and danced round the corpses in her slippered feet. She was grinning, though she still looked drawn and exhausted. She put a bullet through each man's head, two through Jeb Howard's, just to be absolutely certain.

"Nice timing, Eyrie," she crowed, starting towards me. Rabbit fell in line just behind her. "Rabbit bet me you'd show up. I told him this wasn't your scene, but I guess he –"

"Toni!" I yelled, my left arm locking hard to point the Hi-Power.

Her eyebrows furrowed and she started to turn. Stopped when she felt the barrel of Rabbit's gun dig into her neck.

"Drop it," he ordered and she obeyed immediately, letting her weapon fall as if it was hot and burning her fingers.

Rabbit smiled at me over Toni's shoulder. Wasn't fazed by the weapon that I had trained on him.

I heard the passenger door of Mickey's car open, then slam shut.

"What now, Mr Brue?" Rabbit shouted.

I didn't turn, but took a step to the side, keeping the gun on Rabbit, shifting my head slightly in order to cover both angles.

Lewis Brue was out of the car and tearing off the last strands of tape. He had a small knife in his right hand. Must have been hiding it up a sleeve. It never even crossed my mind to properly pat him down. I rid him of his gun in the bookies, thinking that was all I had to worry about. But Brue either kept a knife secreted out of habit, or had foreseen the way this might go and packed the knife especially for the occasion.

Rubbing his hands together to get the circulation flowing, Brue leant against the bonnet and gave the scene a once-over, taking in the corpses, Toni, Rabbit, me.

"Now?" Brue smiled, answering Rabbit's question. "*Now* we tell Eyrie Brown the real story. After all he's been through, and the role he's played in helping us get to this point, I believe he's entitled to it."

And out it all came, the whole damn stinking truth.

FOURTEEN — ANSWERS

"You were on the right track back in the bookies," Brue said, striding across the opening to take the gun from the dead Jeb Howard's hand.

"How so?" I asked as he checked to make sure the gun was still loaded — he'd obviously learnt his lesson earlier.

"Me telling you to leave Toni in your apartment." He tutted. "As if I'd really make a mistake like that."

My eyes narrowed. "You knew Smurf would come for her?"

"Given the number of witnesses in DEL'S, even an idiot like Smurf would have tracked you down eventually," he chuckled, "but I couldn't rely on him to find out your identity and hot-tail it over there in time. He needed a nudge."

I thought it over and let out a deep breath. "You sicced Smurf on her. When I rang and told you all that had happened, you lured me out for a meeting, and at the same time passed my details on to Smurf and sent him over to my place, knowing what he'd find there."

"Guilty as charged," Brue smiled.

"Why?"

"You're smart. Figure it out."

"*Why?*" I shouted, and almost swung my gun on him. Caught myself in time. If I did that, Rabbit would have a clear shot, and I was sure he wouldn't hesitate to take it. I wasn't naïve enough to believe that Brue was telling me all of this for fun, like a big-mouthed Bond villain. He was trying to create an opening, so they could drop me.

"I wanted him to have her," Brue said.

"You bastard," Toni hissed.

Brue shrugged. "Sorry, my dear, but it's a bastard's world."

"You promised you wouldn't double-cross me," I said softly. "When I accepted the job, I warned you not to cross me."

Brue nodded. "And I'm a man of my word. I crossed Toni, not you. I could have left you there for Smurf, but I tempted you out to keep you alive. I thought, when you returned and found her gone, you'd call me with the bad news, then bail. I'd have pretended to curse the fates, thanked you for your help, and that would have been that. I never expected you to pursue her like an action movie hero and get dragged in this deep."

I frowned. "But you offered me more money to continue."

"A scam, to make you believe I truly wanted what was best for her. I knew she'd be gone when you got home, so in the unlikely event that you accepted my offer, I assumed you'd rue the loss and refund the money. I'd have *reluctantly* allowed you to repay me, and again, that would have been that."

"Why call Smurf?" I asked. "Why have one of your own kidnapped and tortured? I thought the idea was to protect her."

"No." Brue's smile faded. "That was never the idea. That was subterfuge, a way to get her into London while maintaining my distance. I wanted to keep her alive until the proper time, but her death was always on the cards. Hers and Howard's."

"I thought you two were close."

"Me and Howard?" He looked surprised.

"You and Toni."

"Oh. Sure." He shrugged. "But like she said, I'm a bastard. I didn't want to kill her, but she was the only way I could get to Jeb Howard, so she was a pawn I had to sacrifice."

"I'm nobody's fucking pawn," Toni spat.

"Yet here you are," Brue said pointedly, then sighed "I was forced to act to get Howard out of the way. Our territories and business interests had overlapped. We were heading for a long, messy war, and I wasn't lying when I said it wasn't a war I could win. One of us had to go.

"I could have kept it basic and paid one of my guys to gun Howard down," Brue continued, "but he's a popular leader, unlike Smurf, and his people would have come looking for revenge. The war I'd been hoping to avoid would have found me regardless. I had to kill him, that was a no-brainer, but I couldn't be linked to his death, so I decided –"

"– to use Toni," I cut in, starting to see how it was meant to play. "An out-of-towner. An old enemy of Howard's. You trick her into coming to London, keeping her link to you a secret from everyone, so it looks like her being here is nothing to do with you. Then you contact Jeb Howard and tell him she's fallen into your lap and you're handing her over to him as a peace offering, but in reality it's an ambush and you let her kill him. Right?"

He tipped an imaginary hat in my direction. "It wasn't quite that simple, but you've got the general gist. The tricky thing was, if anyone knew I'd brought her back or been in contact with her while she was here, it wouldn't work. That's why I had to use a real outsider — *you*. Nobody could trace you to me. It was supposed to look like she came to London just to see Eyrie Brown. People would assume you were lovers or old friends.

"So she hits town, shacks up with you, gets seen in a few places — I told her to keep her head down, but I knew she wouldn't listen. It didn't matter if the people in the dives you took her to didn't know who she was. As long as they saw you together, they'd be able to ID her from photos when Howard's men came asking, as they will, checking their facts, getting everything straight.

"I've a couple of inside men on Howard's crew." Brue sniffed. "No great coup, I'm sure he's got a few among my guys too. They were part of my plan, the only ones who knew what was going on, except for Rabbit, who helped me come up with the scheme in the first place."

"That's what I'm here for," Rabbit snickered, no longer pretending to be just a plain henchman.

"My guys were going to pretend that someone had tipped them off about seeing Toni with you," Brue continued. "They'd have sneaked into your apartment in the dead of night, knocked you out in your sleep – I told them not to kill you, because I really do like you – and made off with Toni. They'd have taken her to Howard, and because he thought they were *his* boys, he wouldn't have been wary. He'd have got up close, to kill her himself. One of my guys would have pulled a knife and slit his throat. Then they'd have gunned down Toni, slipped the knife into her hand and pinned the blame on her."

"Clever little bastard," Toni muttered admiringly.

I knew he was bullshitting when he said he would have had me *knocked out in my sleep*. His men would have killed me, to ensure I couldn't talk. But I figured it would do no harm to let him believe that I believed the lie. The more gullible he assumed I was, the more chance I had of maybe turning the tables on him and getting out of this alive. So I held my tongue and let him rumble on.

"Howard's men would have been shaken," Brue said, "but they knew Toni from way back, how skilled and deadly she was. They'd have been pissed at my guys for not frisking her more effectively, but they'd have believed their story and it would have been dismissed as a freak, unplanned assassination. Howard's successor – a man more open to dialogue and compromise than Jeb – would have taken over. I'd have let a suitable period of mourning pass before opening communications with him, and everything would have been rosy."

"But then Golding Mironova spotted Toni," I murmured, piecing it together as he fed the information to me.

"Right," Brue said.

"And that threw you."

He snorted. "No. *That* was a gift from the heavens. My plan would have worked, but there were holes. Howard's men might have interrogated my guys, demanded to know the name of the person who'd tipped them off. Or they could have gone after you, to determine exactly why Toni had come to London."

That confirmed what I'd suspected, that he couldn't have afforded to let me live, but again I said nothing, not acting as if he'd given himself away.

"My plan was by no means flawless," Brue said humbly. "It was simply the best I could muster, until Golding turned up." He laughed. "I love it when I catch a lucky break. The way things turned out, it looked like Toni had come to London to kill Golding Mironova. It gave her a solid reason to be here. It also meant that my guys could say they'd been at DEL'S, that they'd followed the pair of you back to your place, so there was no need for an imaginary grass."

"Perfect," I sneered. "So why didn't you let them grab her there as planned? Why bring Smurf Mironova into the equation?"

Brue rolled his eyes. "Toni's knife was a weak link. My guys letting her get close to him with a weapon... They're professionals who shouldn't make a mistake of that magnitude. It happens, even with the best of men, and I thought their story would be taken at face value – Toni's always been resourceful, and I was pretty sure they'd accept the fact that she'd simply been a bit sharper than the men who'd brought her in – but it was a risk.

"When you rang to tell me what had happened with Golding, I saw a better way to take out Howard without compromising my guys on the inside. I had to come up with the plan at lightning speed – I had just a vague idea of how it might play out when I was talking with you on the phone, and only properly worked it into shape while you were on your way to meet me – but I've always been quick at thinking on my feet.

"I told my men to stay put, not to target Toni, then rang Smurf Mironova to tell him I knew where the mystery woman's driver lived. I masked my voice, pretended to be a punter from DEL'S, said I wanted revenge for his sister, but also a bag full of cash, which he was to deposit in a bin behind DEL'S — if he made the payment, that's still sitting there, though I doubt he did, cheap little hoodlum that he was.

"I knew Smurf would go crazy when he saw Toni, that he'd drag her away to wreak a terrible revenge — that's the sort of melodramatic thug he was. He never just killed if he could torture first. Once he had her, my guys were going to go to Jeb Howard and tell him a mole had told them she was being held by Smurf. Jeb would have wanted her for himself, so he'd have gone looking to make a trade. My guys would have driven him. Jeb wouldn't have foreseen any problems. The likes of Smurf Mironova always cave in to a man of Jeb Howard's stature.

"My guys would have shot the shit out of Jeb and Smurf at that meeting. Made it look like they'd got into an argument and drawn on one another. They'd have killed Toni too, and anyone else with them. People would have thought Smurf was upset by his sister's death, out of his head on drugs and grief, not thinking clearly. Things got out of hand, probably over something trivial. Bang bang, boom boom, night night. Simple."

I thought it over. It certainly seemed much neater than his original plan, and I guess it would have gone down with Jeb's people as explained. There was only one problem with it...

"I turned up before your guys could make their play," I murmured.

"Yeah." Brue's features darkened. "Where the hell did you get hold of those explosives?"

"I know a man who knows a man," I said lightly.

"Going in there alone... taking them on single-handed..."

I could see he was impressed, and I have to admit I felt fairly good right then, proud of my night's work, even if it had led me to such a sticky end.

"You've watched too many movies," Brue laughed. "Who do you think you are? John Wayne? Bruce Willis? Jackie Chan?"

"Just Eyrie Brown," I replied. "A guy doing his job and earning his pay."

"You fucked my plan up royally," Brue said. "My guys were outside the casino, monitoring the situation, when you hit the scene. When we caught wind of the plan to gang rape Toni, we decided to time it so that they'd contact Howard and bring him in shortly before the action was due to start, which would play even more into our favour — if people thought Smurf was upset that Howard was trying to deny him his sexual payback, it would further justify his apparent wild reaction. They saw you striding out like Clint Eastwood in his heyday, Toni in tow. They didn't know what the fuck was going on, whether to shoot you, help you, follow you or what. They rang me in a panic. I told them to hang back and give me time to think things through again. You'd thrown everything up in the air.

"I could have told my guys to trail you and grab her back, but there was no way they could explain their being at the casino — it wasn't the sort of place they would have hung out, so nobody would have believed that they'd just happened to be there. I could have contacted you, told you to wait somewhere for me, thrown a fake tip-off into the mix, have them pick her up, but I didn't think Jeb's people would buy that after everything else that had gone down. The way I finally saw it, there was only one solution, and it ended up being the best way of them all.

"Betrayal."

"You know all about that," Toni jeered, but Brue ignored her.

"This is where Rabbit proved his true value," Brue said. He looked across at his second in command, who smiled shyly. "Rabbit rang Jeb Howard this afternoon and told him Toni had been in touch, looking for me. Rabbit told Jeb that he'd said I was out of town and it would be a while before I could be contacted, so she'd dealt with him instead. He said she'd told him on the phone that she'd come to kill Golding Mironova, that the hit had gone as planned, but she'd been kidnapped and wounded afterwards. He told Jeb she'd escaped and was in pain and difficulty, that she needed my help and was reaching out.

"Rabbit told Jeb that he'd meant to leave a message for me as soon as he got off the phone to Toni, but then he'd had a thought and paused. And he'd thought some more. And he'd decided to say nothing to me and sell Toni to Jeb instead."

"Was that feasible?" I grunted. "If Rabbit's one of your most trusted men, did you really expect Jeb Howard to believe he'd sell you out?"

"No," Brue smiled, "but the beauty of it was, he was betraying Toni, not me. Massive difference. He made a big show of getting Howard to promise that her execution would remain their secret. I'd hear about her when I got back, try to track her down, but she'd be gone, vanished into thin air, and I'd think she was in hiding or had died in some dark, deserted alley, as long as both men kept quiet."

"They'd be in it together," I nodded. "Rabbit gets rich while appearing to stay loyal to his boss, while Howard gets his woman and nobody ever knows, so there's no fallout to deal with. Both come out of it winners."

"A believable betrayal," Brue chuckled. "Who doesn't try to make a few extra quid on the side when the boss isn't looking, if they think they can do it without bringing the house of cards crashing down?

"We let Jeb choose the location, so he wouldn't think it was a trap. They agreed a price – a sum large enough to make your payoff look like chicken feed – and set a time. The plan, as far as Jeb was aware, was that Rabbit would pick up Toni, tell her he'd arranged for her to see a doctor, but it had to be in the middle of nowhere so that no one would ever find out, then he'd bring her here and hand her over. It was a sweet deal. No reason for Jeb to suspect anything. Hell, if it had been the other way round, *I* would have fallen for it."

I nodded slowly, figuring it would have fooled me too.

"Of course," Brue went on, "in reality Rabbit told Toni that they were going to kill Jeb Howard. As soon as he led her away from us at the bookies, he said that was the reason I'd summoned her, that we'd always planned to play it this way, only without her being kidnapped and tortured."

"I thought nothing of it," Toni said, furious at having been duped. "I couldn't wait to kill that sack of shit. Lewis had used me for similar jobs in the past." She glared at Brue. "Why didn't you just hire me the normal way, let me gun him down and leave it at that? Why screw me like this?"

"Closure," Brue sighed. "I was confident that you and Rabbit would get the drop on Jeb and his boys, but what then? His people would have looked to pin the blame on someone, and I fit the bill too nicely. We had to draw a line beneath this to make it work."

"The plan was for Rabbit to kill you after you'd killed Howard and his men," I told Toni, finding it easy to connect the dots now. "He'd have used Jeb Howard's gun, made it look like you'd shot each other. Then he'd have left his gun in your other hand, so people would have thought you'd gone in solo. It would seem as if everyone present had been killed in the crossfire. Nothing to tie any of it back to Rabbit or Lewis Brue. Right?"

Brue nodded. "And the car they came in was one Rabbit had stolen a few days ago. He'd have simply left it here and walked away."

"All I'd have had to worry about was making it through the East End without having my wallet nicked," Rabbit joked.

"It could have worked," I said, as if I was an expert in such matters.

"It *has* worked," Brue corrected me. "There are the corpses."

"But Toni's still alive," I noted. "And there's me to account for."

Lewis Brue's eyes twinkled. "I'll admit, I didn't bargain on this. I should have kept my mouth shut in the bookies and sent you packing. But I've liked you since you pulled me off the street that blood-spattered night. I didn't want you to feel too bad when you walked away." He grimaced. "Truth be told, I didn't think I'd be dumb enough to let anything slip. You did well to pick up on it, but there should have been nothing to pick up on. My tongue must be loosening in my old age."

I took all that with a large pinch of salt. I think the plan had been for Rabbit to kill me later. That's why Brue had been loose-lipped with me. He saw me as a dead man walking and didn't think he had anything to fear from shooting the breeze with a corpse-in-waiting.

"So where do we go from here?" I asked.

Brue looked surprised. "What do you mean? Nothing has changed. Rabbit will kill Toni – or I might do the honours myself, now that I'm here – and we'll go our merry way."

"You think I'll let that happen?" I was even more surprised than Brue.

"You can't stop it," Brue said. "If you make yourself busy, you'll force us to kill you too, and that's a complication we can do without."

"You're going to kill me anyway," I said, deciding the time had come to stop acting as if I believed his lies about sparing me.

"No," Brue protested firmly.

"Without my corpse, you can't have that closure you so cherish," I said. "Jeb Howard's people will know about me, my connection to Toni, the part I played in rescuing her from Smurf Mironova. They'll come looking for me to find out if I know anything. You can't let me walk away from this."

"Of course I can," Brue disagreed. "Jeb's people won't give a fuck about you. If you stay, sure, they'll be curious to hear your side of the story, and that would be bad for both of us, but they're not going to hunt you if you leave London and never come back. We'll help you slip out of town, set you up with a new identity, point you in the right direction."

I felt a bitter smile dance across my lips. "Back at the bookies, you told me I didn't have to leave London. I guess you wanted to keep me here so that Rabbit could drop by and pay me a visit after he'd finished with Toni, huh?"

"No," he said, but the protest was weaker this time. He knew he'd overplayed his hand, and he knew that I knew it too. "This has all been crazy. So much has happened, and so swiftly. I've had to change course over and over, and I haven't slept all weekend. I'm starting to lose track of what I've said and haven't said, and why I have or haven't said it. If I said in the bookies that you could stay, of course I was wrong, but I have no recollection of that. I must have been rambling."

My scepticism must have shone through because he rolled his eyes dramatically. "OK, I'll admit, it *would* be easier if we added you to the bodies, but I genuinely don't want to do that. I view you as a friend, Eyrie, and I don't discard my friends lightly."

"Toni's your friend and you're discarding *her*," I noted.

He winced but nodded gravely. "Toni's a regrettable sacrifice, one that I'm compelled to make. This just doesn't work without her bullet-riddled corpse."

"Well, you're going to have to find a way to make it work," I insisted, not lowering my gun, even though my arm was aching from having held it aimed for so long.

Brue's eyes narrowed. "I thought nothing happened between you."

"It didn't."

"You sure about that, Eyrie?"

"I'm sure," I said. "It could have, but we didn't let it, because we trusted you and didn't want to betray what we thought was your trust in us."

He sighed. "I'm sorry I let you down," he said, and he sounded on the level.

"I don't want your regrets," I snapped. "I want you to find a way out of this that doesn't involve killing Toni."

He shook his head. "Her death was the one constant in all my plans."

"I don't care," I growled. "It isn't going to happen. I won't let it."

"Of course you will," Brue said with a smile that was several shades colder than any he'd displayed so far. "You've a track record of letting shit like this happen and doing nothing about it."

I stared at him silently, knowing instantly what he was referencing, but amazed that he'd uncovered the secret.

"Did he tell you about the great love of his life?" Brue asked Toni. "The woman he fell in love with when he was in the Army? The terrorist?"

"She wasn't a terrorist," I said automatically.

Brue shrugged. "Whatever. I did my research on you, Eyrie. I couldn't bring you in on something like this without knowing the calibre of man I was involving. It was difficult to get to the core of who you really were and what had happened to make you the man you are, but no lock's impossible to pick if you throw enough money at it."

"He told me about Zahra," Toni said.

"And Jim James?" Brue pressed. "The guy who killed her? Did he tell you about him too?"

"Yes," Toni said.

"Really?" Brue smirked. "He told you what he did to James when he was done crying about his dead girlfriend?"

Uncertainty flickered across Toni's features. "No. I assumed –"

"– that big, brave Eyrie Brown wreaked an unholy revenge," Brue boomed. "It's what you or I would have done. What anyone in our circle would have done." His smile faded and he shot me a look that was half pity, half respect. "But Eyrie's not part of our sick world. He's one of those normal people we hear a lot about but never have much to do with.

"He did nothing," Brue said curtly. "He didn't press charges. He didn't try to kill Jim James. He just walked away, tried to forget about it, returned to civilian life, got drunk every once in a while and howled with madness and grief."

Toni stared at me and I'm not sure if she was sympathetic or scornful.

"That's why you chose me," I croaked. "I didn't stand up to Zahra's killer, so you figured if I somehow pulled through this alive, I wouldn't stand up to Toni's killer either, even if I found out about the betrayal."

"It wasn't the main reason," Brue said, "but it was certainly a factor. Toni's a damn fine looking woman, and no one would describe her as sexually conservative. You stick any straight guy with her for a few days, there's a pretty good chance he'll fall for her. As well as using someone who was an invisible man – as you so aptly put it a while back – I needed someone who wouldn't lose his head and come gunning for revenge if he thought there'd been foul play. No reason you *should* have ever thought that if you'd survived – and as I see you've correctly surmised, that was only an outside chance in my original plan – but I like to cover as many of the angles as I can."

Lewis Brue had been holding the gun he'd retrieved from the slain Jeb Howard by his side. Now he raised it and took aim — not at me but at Toni.

"Rabbit's going to release Toni when I give the word," Brue said, "and I'm going to finish this. Then Rabbit, you, and I are going to leave this place together, as friends."

He cocked an eyebrow at me.

I said nothing.

"You OK with that?" Brue asked.

Again I said nothing, and this time he smiled, self-satisfied.

"Take a step back, Rabbit," Brue said.

Rabbit didn't move. He was eyeing me dubiously.

"He still has me in his sights," Rabbit grunted.

"But his right hand is fucked and he's holding the gun in his left," Brue said. "He wouldn't be able to hit you even if we gave him a dozen tries."

"What if he's left-handed?" Rabbit asked.

"He's not," Brue said. "I saw him using his right hand back at the start of our adventure, when he was personalising the bank account that I set him up with."

"I dunno..." Rabbit wasn't cool with this.

"Are you ambidextrous, Eyrie?" Brue jokingly asked.

"No," I replied honestly.

"There you go," he said to Rabbit, but Rabbit was still reluctant to chance it. Brue muttered something to himself, then snapped at me, "Lower your gun."

I glanced at him as if I wasn't sure what he'd said.

"Come on," Brue said encouragingly. "We can't proceed until you prove you're on the same page as us. We need a show of good faith."

I kept my Hi-Power trained on Rabbit, but I started blinking nervously.

"The sooner you put your gun down, the sooner we can wrap this up and be out of here," Brue said softly, kindly, like he was trying to do me a favour. "Let's finish this, put our weapons away, and go get drunk."

My hand trembled and I began to lower the gun. Caught Toni's eye. She looked resigned. No hatred in her expression. This was just the way things played out in her world. She didn't blame me for going along with Lewis Brue and saving my own neck. It's what she would have done in my position.

I let the gun dip further and looked aside with a heavy, defeated sigh.

"Now," Brue said, and Rabbit released Toni and took a step back. He took a second step. A third.

That's when my trembling hand steadied and flashed up, and I fired.

The slug smashed through Rabbit's teeth and tore out the back of his skull. He flopped to the ground, his face a bloody facsimile of what it had been a mere second before.

I spun towards a shocked Lewis Brue and fired again. The bullet struck him in his right shoulder and his gun went flying as he was knocked backwards. Brue roared with pain and shock as he clutched the wound with his left hand and gawped at me, too stunned to try racing for cover.

"Are you crazy?" he shouted as a dazed Toni blinked at Rabbit, then at me, then at Rabbit again, not quite sure what had just gone down. "Are you out of your fucking mind?"

"No," I said, advancing slowly.

"It makes no sense," he croaked, staring at Rabbit's corpse, then at his bleeding hand. "Leopards don't change their spots. You did nothing before. You should have done nothing again."

I shook my head. "I'm surprised you found out as much as you did about me, but you should have dug deeper. You've been operating under a misperception."

"What are you talking about?" he cried.

"I did try to kill Dancing James in the desert," I said. "But he expected that and was ready for me. I was easily subdued and the chance for immediate retribution passed before I could claim it."

"But you've had years since then," Brue bellowed. "You could have gone after him but didn't. You let him get away with it. He's still alive — I checked. You…"

He stopped, his expression changing as an awful understanding set in. A glance in Toni's direction told me that she understood too. She was no longer blinking dumbly. Instead a small, admiring smile had lifted the corners of her mouth.

"I've been waiting," I said softly. "I had a lot of time to think and I made up my mind to hurt him the way he'd hurt me. I decided to get away with it too. Not because I value my life, but because Zahra wouldn't have wanted me to spend decades in gaol.

"Dancing James bailed from the Army a couple of years after I did," I continued, "and I've kept tabs on him ever since. He had a rough time of it in the beginning, so I let him be. I wasn't interested in killing him when he was down and out. I hoped he'd build a life for himself and fall in love. I was never going to let him have children – I don't want to rob a child of a father – but I wanted him to experience everything else, so that I could take it all away from him. I plan to give him a few moments when I'm killing him, to reflect on all that he's lost and feel the pain that I felt when he took all that away from me."

I smiled grimly and said with hawkish relish, "He's almost there. He drifted from one job and relationship to another for a long time, longer than I would have liked – I was often tempted to take him out, especially when I'd been drinking – but he's settled down, found a woman who loves him, and gainful employment. I'll give it another year, to let him get *really* comfortable. Then I'll make my move."

"Son of a bitch," Brue gasped. "I got you all wrong, didn't I?"

"On so many levels," I said, and tapped my left hand with my bloodied right. "I'm not ambidextrous, and as you saw when I was using your phone, I *am* right-handed. But if you'd got to know me better before you set out to screw me, you would have learnt that I fought *southpaw*. When it comes to boxing, using a tool, shooting a gun... I'm just as good with my left hand as my right."

He chuckled and applauded softly, sarcastically. Then his face hardened. "I was wrong about something else too. You *are* part of my world, a killer just like me and Toni."

"Yeah," I said bleakly. "The difference is, I don't want to be. But I'll kill if I have to. If I must. I'll kill for love."

"Don't do this, Eyrie," Brue said as I took careful aim. "We can recalculate, pin the blame on Rabbit, make him the fall guy. You, me and Toni can all walk free."

"I don't think so."

He smiled desperately. "You don't trust me?"

"It's not that. But if you and Rabbit are found here, next to the other corpses, nobody's going to ask any questions at all."

The last few patches of colour drained from his face and he began breathing heavily.

"There's nothing to connect me and Toni to this," I carried on. "Apart from your insiders on Jeb Howard's team – who won't say a word, because they can't talk without condemning themselves – nobody knows you brought Toni to London. In the eyes of the world, we were never here and had nothing to do with this. And with you, Jeb Howard and Rabbit dead, and your insiders tied to silence by their complicity, there's no reason why anyone should ever think otherwise."

"Wait a minute," he croaked. "Let's not rush this. We can talk."

"No," I said. "We're done talking. All that's left now is..." I smiled grimly and framed the word carefully. "*Closure.*"

"You don't know what you're getting into," he warned. "You can't kill a man like me and just waltz away into the night."

"But I'm not killing you," I said. "Jeb Howard is. At least that's how it'll look once I wipe my prints from this gun and stick it in his hand."

"I'll pay you," he moaned. "Name your price. I'll give you whatever you want."

"He doesn't have a price, fucknuts," Toni snarled, stepping up beside me. "And even if he did, you couldn't buy off *me*." She had recovered her gun and was shaking furiously. She took aim.

"No," I said softly. "This one's mine."

"You sure?" she asked.

"Yeah. I warned him not to double-cross me. Told him what I'd do if he did."

"Mother of fuck." Brue spat into the dirt by his feet. He could see his death in my eyes. He smiled shakily, trying to depart this world as manfully as he could. "Can I at least have a couple of minutes to make my peace with God?" he quipped.

I shot him between the eyes. He fell and was still. The sound took longer to die than he did.

"No," I said.

FIFTEEN — THE PAYOFF

There were practicalities to tend to before we did anything else.

First, Toni determined that the bullet that had struck my arm was lodged inside. She said that was a good thing, as otherwise we'd have had to go scouting around for it, and there was little chance we would have found it in the dark. If we'd left it behind, the forensics team would have discovered it and ID'd my blood when they tested it, and I'd have been implicated. This way, I was carrying it away within me, and Toni said she knew a doctor up north who could extract and dispose of it discreetly.

Next, Toni bandaged my arm to stop the bleeding, then swiftly but expertly cleaned the area where I'd been standing, to ensure I left no incriminating bloodstains.

After that we palmed off our guns on Lewis Brue and Rabbit, then wiped Rabbit's car of prints.

I would have left at that stage, but Toni, practical to the end, went looking for the money that Jeb Howard had brought to pay the fake traitor, Rabbit. She found it in the back of the limo. Two bags so full of cash that it would take a couple of days to count.

I can't deny that, despite everything that had happened, both of us stood there for a minute, staring down at the money, grinning like kids.

Toni winced as she picked up the bags.

"Are your hands OK?" I asked.

"They will be," she sighed. "Come on. We need to make tracks."

Those were the last words we exchanged for a few hours, until we were out of London and heading north. I drove slowly, the pain in my arm keeping me alert despite my deep weariness, thinking about the two men I'd killed, looking ahead to the time when I'd have to kill again.

The killing hadn't given me a buzz, just as thoughts of claiming my revenge on Dancing James had never set me tingling. I didn't think I'd have bad dreams about this. Didn't think the faces of the dead men would haunt my thoughts for years to come. The way I saw it, when shit needs taking care of, you take care of it, and try not to let the stink get to you too much.

We stopped at a tourist spot on the edge of a valley. Got out of the car and sat on a bench. It was quiet, the sun dipping out of sight, a few pink clouds trailing across the horizon. Toni was shivering — we still hadn't sorted her out with socks and shoes, just those cheap slippers I'd bought in the shop. I took off my jacket and draped it round her shoulders. Let my hands rest there. She covered them with her own.

"What now?" she asked quietly.

I looked at the clouds.

"I'm not sure," I admitted.

"The money will make it easier," she assured me.

I edged forward to face her directly. "What about you and me?"

It was her turn to look uncertain. "I don't know."

"Do you want to split the cash and go our separate ways?" I pressed.

"Do you?" she countered.

"No," I whispered.

"Me neither," she whispered back. "But…"

I felt my stomach tighten. "*But...?*" I echoed.

"We hardly know anything about each other," she said, staring at me with dark, scared eyes. "We shared some stuff back at the docks, sure, but do you really think we could make this work long-term?"

I smiled. "I'm willing to find out if you are."

She gulped, looking very young and innocent all of a sudden. "I'm willing too, but I know you're going to go after that guy one day, Dancing James, and that will be risky, no matter how well you plan it."

"Maybe you can help me with that," I said, half joking.

"Sure I can," she said, all serious. "The point I'm making is, if you don't hook up with me, that's the only thing like this you'll ever have to face. Once you're done with James, you can lead a normal life."

"You think I can't do that with you?" I asked softly.

"I know you can't," she said sadly. "Normality isn't my world, hasn't been for a long time now."

"Maybe I can help you find it again," I said.

"No," she snapped, "and you're a fool if you think that's going to happen, that you can change me. I'm trouble, Eyrie Brown."

"Don't I know it," I chuckled.

"I'll get bored," she said. "I'll want action."

"I won't try to restrain you."

"I can be Hell itself when I'm in a bad mood."

"I noticed."

"We can never return to London."

"I had no plans to return anyway."

"I can't cook."

"We can afford to eat out."

"I'm messy, a real pig."

"I'll clean up after you."

"What if we don't gel in the sack? We haven't even kissed. We might not be compatible."

I smiled. "Only one way to find out."

I stood and picked her up, cradling her in my arms the way I had when I'd rescued her from Smurf Mironova's.

"What about what those bastards at Smurf's did to me?" she asked, tears in her eyes. "They shamed me, for the world to see."

"That was their shame, not yours. It doesn't bother me."

"And the killing?" she moaned, tears rolling down her cheeks, some of hope, more of fear that those hopes would be dashed. "It doesn't bother you that I've killed so often, that I think so little of life and other people's right to it?"

"Well, you know what a wise man once said," I murmured, tilting her so the glow of the setting sun was in her hair, letting her see my grin before bending to kiss her for the first time, knowing the exact words I needed to tie up all the loose ends and start us on the next leg of what would hopefully be a long and joyous journey together. *"Nobody's perfect..."*

THE END

this book was heated up from cold between 10th june 1996 and 3rd december 2019

Printed in Great Britain
by Amazon